MW00932680

DINGED

Also by Tommy Greenwald

Game Changer

Rivals

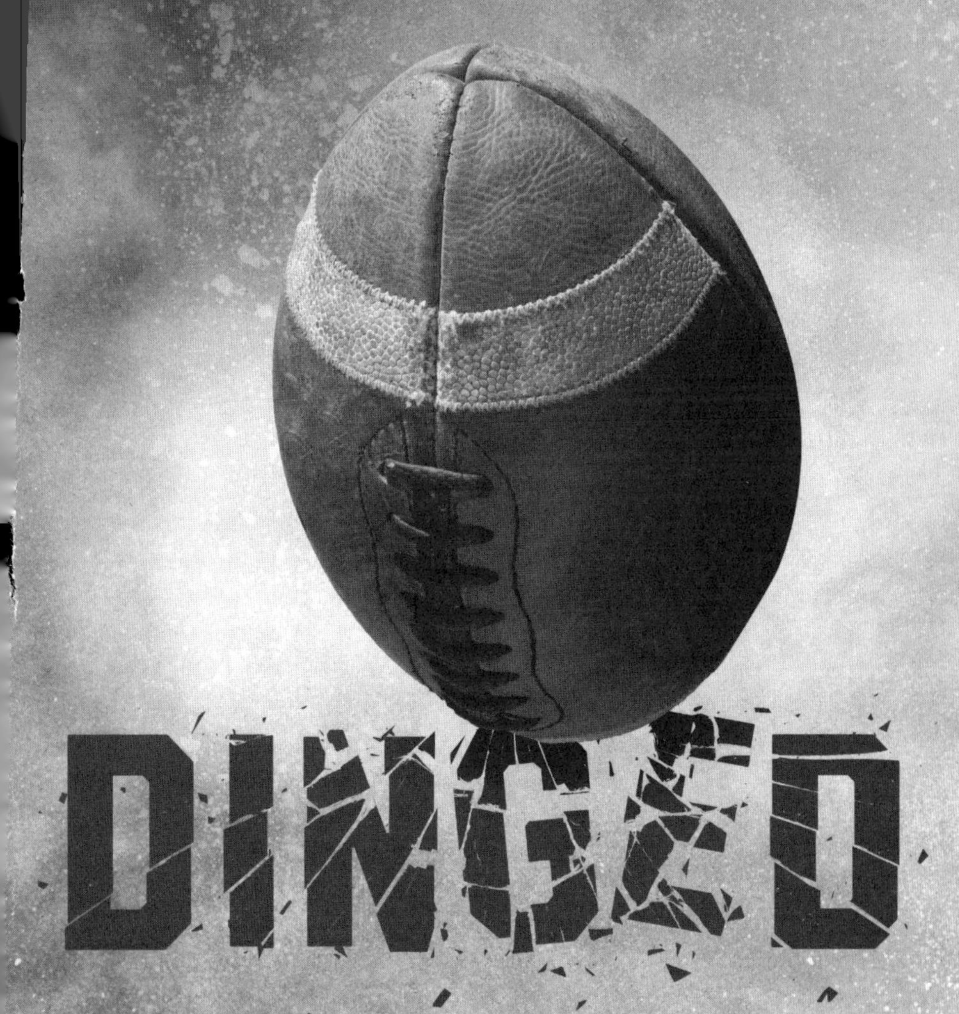

DINGED

TOMMY GREENWALD

AMULET BOOKS • NEW YORK

PUBLISHER'S NOTE: This is a work of fiction. Names, characters, places, and incidents are either the product of the author's imagination or used fictitiously, and any resemblance to actual persons, living or dead, business establishments, events, or locales is entirely coincidental.

Cataloging-in-Publication Data has been applied for and may be obtained from the Library of Congress.

ISBN 978-1-4197-5515-6

Title page art by Neil Swaab
Book design by Chelsea Hunter

Printed and bound in China

10 9 8 7 6 5 4 3

ABRAMS The Art of Books
195 Broadway, New York, NY 10007
abramsbooks.com

To the memory of Mike Webster

In American football getting "dinged" equates to moments of dizziness, confusion, or grogginess that can follow a blow to the head. There are approximately 100,000 to 300,000 concussive episodes occurring in the game of American football each year.

It is now known that those instances of mild concussion or "dings" that we may have previously not noticed could very well be causing progressive neurodegenerative damage to a player's brain. Symptoms [. . .] may begin years or decades later and include a progressive decline of memory, as well as depression, poor impulse control, suicidal behavior, and, eventually, dementia similar to Alzheimer's disease.

Given the millions of athletes participating in contact sports that involve repetitive brain trauma, [this] represents an important public health issue. In the future, focused and intensive study of the risk factors could potentially uncover methods to prevent and treat this disease.

—United States National Library of Medicine

PROLOGUE

I live for the game.

How could I not?

My dad lived for the game before me. It made him rich and famous. And when he discovered I had talent—really rare talent, according to pretty much everyone I've ever met—he made it his life's mission to help me become as good as I could be.

My mom had no choice but to go along for the ride, but she loves it, too. The game scares her, sure, but I know the pride she feels. The pride of knowing her husband made it to the top, and of knowing that her only son is probably going to make it there, too.

So yeah, I was destined to play football pretty much before I was born.

But don't get me wrong.

It's not like anybody is forcing me to do anything I don't want to do.

Because I love it.

I love every bit of it.

I love the competition, the teamwork, the beauty, the brutality, how it's so simple and so complicated at the same time, how it's the one thing that makes me feel truly alive.

And sure—I love being better than everyone else.

So like I said . . . I live for the game.

I guess the question is:

Am I willing to die for it?

PART I

Clouds

WALTHORNENEWS.COM

WELCOME TO THE JUNGLE
A HIGH SCHOOL SPORTS BLOG ABOUT
THE WALTHORNE WILDCATS
BY ALFIE JENKS
MONDAY, SEPTEMBER 7

High School Football Hopes Rest on Freshman Phenom's Shoulders

William Toffler has been coaching football a long time—more than 25 years, by his count. So he knows what it's like to come across a once-in-a-generation talent.

Enter Caleb Springer.

"This is a special kid," Coach Toffler says. "We're super lucky to have him." Caleb, only 14 years old and a rising freshman at Walthorne High School, has been wowing people with his quarterbacking skills since his days playing for the Peewee Panthers as a six-year-old. And it's no wonder: Caleb's father, Sammy Springer, played in the NFL for seven years and was an all-pro wide receiver.

Coach Toffler, who has done a great job since replacing the legendary Hall of Famer Louis Bizetti as Head Football Coach at Walthorne High two years ago, has already made clear he plans on starting Caleb right away. "This isn't a kid who needs to wait his turn," says Coach Toffler. "His poise and ability are way beyond his years. I don't want to put too much pressure on the kid, but we expect to compete for the state title with Caleb at the helm. He's ready to go."

Meanwhile, Caleb's dad is excited to see his son's high school debut. "Oh, you bet, we've been waiting for this for a long time," said Sammy Springer. "Seeing my boy out there playing high school football is a dream come true." When asked if he was upset that his son didn't play wide receiver like him, the former NFL star laughed. "Are you kidding? No one gets hit harder than the little guys on the outside. He'll be a lot safer back there in the pocket, being protected by the big boys on the line."

You can see Caleb Springer's high school debut for yourself this Friday night at home against Meadow Ridge.

WWHS
WALTHORNE HIGH SCHOOL RADIO

ALFIE: Testing, testing, 123 . . .
Testing . . .
Is this thing on?

CALEB: Well, you're blasting through my headphones, so I guess yes.

ALFIE: Sweet! And oh, uh, sorry about the levels. Still getting used to this new equipment.

CALEB: Cool. This is all new for me, too.

ALFIE: Okay, so, yeah! Welcome to my first-ever high school edition of "Talking Sports" on WWHS. This is Alfie Jenks, associate sports editor.

CALEB: Wait, are you a freshman, too? Or should I say freshwoman?

ALFIE: Ha. Neither. I'm a sophomore—they don't let you host your own show till you're a sophomore.

CALEB: Oh cool, well, congrats on your first show.

ALFIE: Yeah, thanks! So, anyway, yeah, I'm here with Caleb Springer, who *is* an actual freshman, and who has just been named the first-string quarterback of the Walthorne High Wildcats. We've got a really exciting season coming up, starting with the first game this Friday night against Meadow Ridge. So, Caleb, are you ready to go?

CALEB: I sure hope so.

ALFIE: Do you feel, like, a lot of pressure because you're so good?

CALEB: Well, uh, thanks, I guess, but I don't know about that—

ALFIE: You are, though. You're, like, the best quarterback Walthorne has ever had. Everyone says so. And you're only a freshman. How does that feel? Does it feel awesome?

CALEB: Oh man.

ALFIE: Does it, like, stress you out? Or how about the fact that your dad was a famous player in the NFL? Is that a lot of pressure, too?

CALEB: He's not that fam—

ALFIE: Oh shoot, wait, hold on a sec. I forgot something. Mr. Rashad says reporters always need to make sure our readers or listeners understand the background.

CALEB: Who?

ALFIE: My advisor, Mr. Rashad. So, uh, for all you listeners out there, Caleb's dad is Sammy Springer, who played for the New York Jets and was, like, this amazing wide receiver and had this incredible career and made it into the Pro Football Hall of Fame.

CALEB: Actually, that's not quite true. I mean, the Jets part is true, and the wide receiver part is true. He played in the pros for seven years, but he isn't in the Pro Football Hall of

Fame. He's in the College Football Hall of Fame, though.

ALFIE: Oh, my bad! Why only seven years?

CALEB: Uh, well, that's actually longer than most NFL players play. They get banged up, you know—injuries and stuff.

ALFIE: Oh man. Injuries suck.

CALEB: They sure do. Can you say "suck" on the radio?

ALFIE: Uh . . . I'm not sure, to be honest. I better . . . This has been "Talking Sports," with associate sports editor Alfie Jenks, signing off.

◂1

Walthorne High vs. Meadow Ridge High
Season Record: 0–0

Buck helps block out the noise.

When I first started playing football, my dad told me that my helmet was going to be my best friend, so I should give it a name. I named it Buck. I can't remember why. I've had a lot of helmets since then, and they've all been Buck.

My friends think it's dumb, but I don't care.

Buck's main job is to protect my head, of course. High school football crowds can be loud, though—really loud—and thanks to Buck, it's more like a low buzzing. It's always there, but it's far away.

I like it that way. It helps me think.

One of the things I love most about football is how much you have to think. Who does what, who goes where, split-second decisions, when to run, when to pitch, when to hand off, when to throw, who to throw to, how to throw it, should I throw it high and soft, low and hard, which hole to hit, which blocker to run behind—that's all stuff you have to think about on pretty much every play.

Everyone thinks football is just people smashing into other people, but it's actually a lot more than that.

Although there is plenty of smashing.

At the end of the first quarter, we're up 14–0. I throw a nineteen-yard pass to Ethan Metzger in the corner of the end zone for the first touchdown. On the second score, I get a great block from Kenny Coleman—an offensive lineman and the only other freshman on varsity—and I basically walk in from twelve yards out.

We huddle up on the sideline. I hear Coach Toffler talking, but I'm only half-listening. I know what to do. I have an instinct for the game that's pretty foolproof. My dad calls it a sixth sense. The coaches know it and leave me alone. So yeah, I'm not really paying attention. Instead, I'm staring across the field, at the Meadow Ridge players.

I know what I'm looking for.

The sag.

That's what my dad calls it. "The sag." It's when the players on the other team lose their confidence. Their shoulders drop, they run back to the huddle with less energy, their yells of encouragement to their teammates are a little less loud. My dad says there's a moment in every game when one team sags. Sometimes it's in the first quarter, sometimes it's after the last play of the game. When you see it in the other team, you know you've got them—it's "the final nail in the coffin," as my coaches like to say. But when you see it in your own team, it's up to you to straighten out your teammates. Because the sag is the difference between winning and losing. Between sleeping well and tossing and turning.

Between life and death.

"BRING IT IN!" hollers our captain, this really big dude named Ron Johnson. We huddle up—the whole team, all forty-eight of us.

Ron is screaming at the top of his lungs. "WE STILL GOT WORK TO DO! NO LETUP! THESE GUYS ARE TOUGH! WE NEED TO PUT THEM AWAY!"

While Ron is pumping us up, I'm still looking over at the Meadow Ridge sideline, trying to find the sag. I notice this one kid, number 72. Man, that dude is huge. I gotta make sure he doesn't touch so much as a hair on my—

"SPRINGER! SPRINGER, WHAT ARE YOU DOING? ARE YOU EVEN LISTENING?"

Ron is staring straight at me, which means the rest of the team is, too.

"Uh, yeah, nothing, Ron. Just thinking about the game."

"Well, how about thinking about the TEAM, Mr. Greatest QB Ever! Circle it up with the REST OF US NOW!"

I do as I'm told, of course. Ron is the captain, he's a senior, and he plays center, which means he's in charge of protecting me. But the thing is, even though he's a great high school player, Ron knows he's not quite big enough for major college football, so when I came along with all the attention, it kind of got him pissed off. And he hasn't stopped being pissed off about it since.

"Sorry about that, Ron," I say. "Won't happen again."

Ron gives a satisfied grunt, then resumes his hollering. "LET'S KEEP THE PRESSURE ON! WILDCATS ON THREE! ONE, TWO, THREE . . ."

"WILDCATS!"

⁂

We take the field for the second quarter. It's our ball, and we're on the Meadow Ridge thirty-seven yard line and marching. Soon it's gonna be 21–0 and I'm going to look for the sag again, and this time I bet I'll find it.

Sports is all about confidence, right?

That's another one of my dad's favorite phrases. He says it all the time.

Sports is all about confidence. And you know what else is? Life. Life is all about confidence. Believing in yourself is half the battle. That's just the way it is.

I'm thinking about that, and about how once we score this touchdown, Meadow Ridge is going to realize it's the beginning of the end. I'm thinking about my dad and that smile he gives me after a good game, and the hug my mom is going to give me when she says what she always says after every game. *Thank God you're okay.*

And I'm thinking about Nina, even though she's not here. If I'm lucky, she'll show up after the game ends. She can't stand football. She calls it disgusting and barbaric, and thinks it should be illegal.

That's one reason people find it so hard to believe we like each other.

But you know what? My hunch is that even though Nina says

she hates football, and part of her definitely does, there's another part of her that thinks it's cool to be dating the hotshot quarterback.

She would never admit that, of course. Never in a million years.

I'm thinking about all that stuff—Nina, and my mom and dad, and waiting for the kids from Meadow Ridge to sag—instead of what I should be thinking about, which is the play we're about to run.

I yell, "HUT!"

We're running an option play, meaning I can either run the ball or pitch it to our tailback, Mitch Sellers. He's wide open, and his hands are outstretched, waiting, but I lose my concentration for a fraction of a second, and I hesitate, and by the time I decide to pitch to him, he's covered, so I have no choice but to keep the ball and turn upfield, and right as I shift my body, I see the giant kid, number 72, who's pretty quick, and he's bearing down on me, and I try to turn away, but I just end up swinging my head right toward his left shoulder pad, and I close my eyes and wait for the impact, and it comes, *CRASH*—no, more like CRASH!!!—and it feels like Buck crumples up like a Coke can, and I hear a ringing sound that gets louder and louder and then softer and softer . . .

WWHS
WALTHORNE HIGH SCHOOL RADIO
TRANSCRIPT OF PLAY-BY-PLAY
ALFIE JENKS AND JULIAN HESS

ALFIE: Whoa! That was some hit! Caleb Springer decided to keep the ball on the option play and was met head-on by number 72 on Meadow Ridge, Jerrod Clemmons.

JULIAN: Ouch! That looked like it hurt.

ALFIE: I don't know about that decision by Caleb there—he's usually really smart about that kind of stuff.

JULIAN: Yep, he looked like me in algebra class. Completely lost.

ALFIE: Just a really hard hit, but Caleb is a tough kid and I'm sure he won't make that mistake again.

JULIAN: If he does, we're going to need some superglue out here to stick his head back onto his shoulders.

ALFIE: You're using some very colorful phrases today, Julian.

JULIAN: Thanks!

ALFIE: Anyway, that brings up a third and two at the Meadow Ridge thirty-nine yard line . . .

⁂

. . . and I see those bright lights that you can see even when your eyes are shut really tight, and their reflections shoot through my head like I have eyes everywhere that follow the bright lights around, and I know I'm lying down even though I can't really feel the ground, no, wait, I'm standing up, no, I was right the first time, I'm lying down, and the only thing I can hear is my breath, and I open my eyes and slowly noise comes back, then I see feet around me, and someone is bending over but I'm not sure who.

"Caleb?" It's Kenny. "You good?"

"Yup," I say. "Buck saved my ass."

Kenny puts out his two hands, and I grab them and try to hop up. The hop is important, it shows you're okay, you're tough, you're good to go. I feel myself wobble for a second, but Kenny steadies me so quickly, I don't think anyone notices. I look over at the sidelines and give them a thumbs-up, then run back to the huddle. I'm not going to give anyone a chance to think about whether or not I should stay in the game.

I'm okay and that's all there is to it.

We huddle up. It takes me a few seconds to focus. I wait for someone to bring in the play from the sidelines. Everyone is looking at me, waiting for me to say something.

"You sure you're okay?" Ron asks. "That dude clocked you for real."

I'm not sure if Ron saw me wobble, but I know this much: There's no way I'm telling the captain of the team I'm not okay. You don't do that in football. I give Ron a quick nod. He gladly decides to believe me. The new play comes in. I bark it out to the team. We clap our hands and break the huddle.

Four plays later, we score.

Meadow Ridge sags.

We end up winning, 46–6.

2

As soon as the coach finishes his postgame speech, I head off to find my parents.

It's been that way since the first game I ever played.

When I get to my mom, she grabs my head with her hands. "Thank God you're okay." She's been around football ever since college, when she met my dad, and she loves it, or she's learned to love it, and she loves the life it's given our family.

My dad is where he always is—leaning against the bleachers, waiting. Most of the dads stick together during the games, screaming and hollering, smacking each other on the back after wins, congratulating each other, trying not to brag about their own sons but bragging anyway, finding their sons afterward and high-fiving them, taking group pictures, and stuff like that. My dad doesn't do any of that. He prefers to watch the games quietly, off to the side, with my mom. He waits for people to come to him. He's always waited for people to come to him—even his own son.

When I reach him, he gives me a hug—he's still the

strongest person I've ever met, so his hugs hurt—and a big smile. Then he sticks out his hand and I shake it—a formal handshake, like always.

"Way to bring it, Cae," he says, calling me by my nickname.

"Thanks, Dad."

"You looked really sharp out there. Really sharp! Freshman QB, I mean, come on!" He tries not to show it, but I can tell how proud he is of me, and how happy he is that his son is a good football player. That's another reason why I love the game so much.

I try to keep my voice even and cool. "Yeah, it was fun."

My dad bellows out a loud laugh. "Fun? FUN? Dude, you rocked it!" Then he takes a step back and gives me a once-over. "You get rung up a little bit, though?"

My mom frowns. "Rung up?"

My dad immediately makes light of it. "Rung up, honey. You know, like getting your bell rung. Just a little knock, that's all."

She grabs my hand and twirls me toward her. "What happened, Caleb?"

"Nothing, Ma. I'm fine."

"Was it that sack in the second quarter? Did something

happen there?" My mom's eyes search the field, which is always crowded right after games. I know who she's looking for—Coach Toffler.

But my dad grabs her hand, lowering his voice, because he knows a lot of people are watching him. He's used to it. People have been watching him since he was in high school. Kind of like the way they're starting to watch me. "Honey, we're good," he tells my mom. "Caleb is fine. You think I would let anything happen to our boy? He's fine. It was one play. All good. Trust me."

My mom nods. "I do trust you, hon." She knows there are some arguments she can't win.

"Caleb," my dad says, "there's someone I want you to meet."

He nods at another man, talking to a few Walthorne fans. I'd noticed him during the game. He's hard not to notice. The guy is huge. Like, medium-sized-building huge.

"This is Brandon Williams," my dad says. "We played pro ball together."

I can feel other people listening to us while pretending not to. I'm used to it because of my dad, but now, with another ex-NFL player added to the mix, it becomes even more obvious.

Brandon Williams sticks out his massive hand, and I shake it nervously. He laughs. "Don't worry, kid, I'm not gonna mess with that hand of yours. It's attached to a million-dollar arm."

My dad grins. "Brandon was a hell of a D-lineman back in the day, and now he's on the coaching staff up at State. His job is to evaluate and recruit talent, and he likes what he sees."

I'm not sure what my dad is talking about.

Brandon sees my confusion and laughs. "Easy, Dinger, you're freaking the kid out." Dinger is my dad's nickname from his playing days, I guess because it rhymes with Springer. "No one's talking about recruiting a fourteen-year-old kid. But your boy has some serious talent, that's for sure."

Brandon bends down to about half his height so he can whisper something in my mom's ear. Then he looks back to me.

"Hey, kid," he says, "you want to join me at a game up at State in a few weeks? We got Auburn coming in, should be a dogfight. You can watch the game from the coaches' booth, then I'll take you down to the locker room after the game and show you around. You can meet the guys and get a feel for what it's like to play big-time college football. What do you say?"

I look at my dad, who nods and grins. I tell Brandon, "That sounds amazing, thank you."

Some part of me knows that what's happening right now is important. My heart races. I'm trying to understand everything that's going on, which is hard, because people are pounding me on the back and saying good game, and I don't want to admit it but my head is still hurting a little bit, it's been hurting ever since number 72 clocked me, and everything feels really loud even though it probably isn't, and this gigantic guy who played with my dad is basically telling me that he wants me to start thinking about playing football at the college where he coaches, and it's all a lot to process, which might be why I don't think anything of it when my dad starts laughing.

After a few seconds, though, I realize it's not his typical laugh, the one that makes everyone feel good.

This laugh sounds a little off.

"What about me?" he asks.

We all look at him.

"What do you mean?" my mom asks.

My dad blinks a few times. "Aren't I invited?"

My mom and I look at each other. Ordinarily, we would both think Dad was joking around, but there's something about the way he's acting that makes us not sure.

Neither of us speaks.

Brandon does, though. "Dinger? Buddy? You're kidding, right?"

My dad's face turns red. Really red. But then, just as suddenly, he takes a deep breath and the redness fades. "HA! Of course I'm kidding! This is going to be spectacular, my boy getting a chance to check out the football program up at State, with my absolute favorite teammate of all time showing him around!" A flash of concern crosses his face. "I can come, though, right? It's okay if I come?"

Brandon puts his hand on my dad's shoulder. "You are too much, Dinger. We wouldn't dream of doing it without you, buddy. Right, Caleb?"

"Of course not!" I say, but I'm completely confused. Is it possible my dad actually thought he wasn't invited?

"Ready to go, Sammy?" my mom asks.

My dad grabs her hand and gives her a quick kiss on the cheek. "In a minute, Cath. Just going to go congratulate the coach on the game." As he walks off, the crowd automatically parts for him, creating a path as he walks toward Coach Toffler. The two greet each other with a big hug, like long-lost brothers, and immediately start yapping away.

My mom watches and shakes her head. "Wow, does your dad love football."

"That's because it's the greatest game ever invented," I tell her.

"I couldn't agree more, Caleb," Brandon says. "And that passion you have for the game? You can't teach that. It's another thing that's going to help you become something very special in this game."

"Thank you, sir."

"Ha! No calling me sir!"

My mom laughs, and as she and Brandon start chatting, more people come up and congratulate me on the game, including my two best friends, Eric Stetler and Jamie Chu.

"Awesome game, dude!" Eric says.

"Amazing how comfortable you looked out there," Jamie says.

"Thanks, guys," I say. "It felt pretty sweet, I gotta admit."

"Hey, someone told me the varsity games are, like, livestreamed now," Jamie says. "So that means you were shredding it for millions watching at home."

Eric turns to Jamie. "Wait, so your JV games aren't livestreamed?"

Jamie responds by punching Eric in the shoulder.

"Next year it'll be you catching my passes," I tell Jamie.

"We'll see," Jamie mumbles.

"No, for real!"

Eric makes a goofy face. "And I'll stick my nose in the camera and say, 'I've known those guys since second grade!'"

As we all laugh, I see Nina waving at me from the parking lot. "Yeah, anyway you guys, I gotta roll," I say.

"Wait, seriously?" Eric turns and sees Nina. "Oh, gotcha," he adds, looking a little bummed.

I turn to my dad's college-coach friend. "It was an honor to meet you, Mr. Williams."

"The pleasure is mine," he says. "I'll see you in a few weeks, and we'll have ourselves a time!"

I start walking up to the parking lot as quickly as I can without running. After a few steps, I no longer care about ditching my best friends, or the fact that I just met a guy who might be recruiting me for college.

A girlfriend can do that to a guy.

3

Nina has a big camera around her neck that is really old, and is wearing a shirt with a picture of Eleanor Roosevelt on it. When I first saw her wearing that shirt about a year ago, I didn't know who Eleanor Roosevelt was. I do now, though.

She gives me a giant exaggerated smile. "There he is! The superstar! What an amazing game! You ran so fast and threw the ball so far and everything!"

I know she's being sarcastic, because she wasn't even at the game. She likes to come after to take pictures, but I'm pretty sure she's never seen me play. But I don't care. I take my helmet off and hug her.

She peers down at my hands. "The fact that you named that thing Buck is truly the most ridiculous thing I've ever heard."

"Thank you for saying that," I say, "because I didn't hear you the first ten thousand times you said it."

She laughs, then gets up on her tiptoes and gives me a kiss on the cheek.

I can feel people watching.

I whisper something to her that I don't have the nerve to tell anyone else. "My head hurts."

Nina frowns. "What do you mean?"

"I got hit pretty good."

I see clouds pass through her eyes. "This game," she says, practically spitting. "This freakin' game. I mean, seriously."

"It was just one play."

"I don't care!" She throws her hands up in the air. "I gotta go."

"You just got here."

"I can't be here right now. Text me later."

"Nina, wait!"

But she doesn't wait. She waves goodbye without looking back. I glance around, wondering who noticed that exchange, who saw the star quarterback get dissed by his girlfriend, but all of a sudden no one is paying attention.

People are too smart to get caught.

⁂

On the way home, we stop at Dusty's, which has the best ice cream you've ever eaten in your life.

“What did you and Coach talk about?” I ask my dad, between licks of my coffee cone.

“Just wanted to make sure he knew that you’d taken a little shot,” my dad says, meaning the hit I took. Then he winks at my mom. “I let him know that your mother was keeping a close eye on him and was ready to pounce in order to protect her baby boy.”

My mom doesn’t look all that amused, though. “You need to be responsible for yourself, too,” she tells me. “If you ever take a hard hit and don’t feel right, you need to come out of the game. You have to say something. Tell the coach, tell the captain, tell someone. Right away.”

“She’s absolutely right,” my dad says. “There’s no shame in saying you’re hurt. You’re in this for the long haul. If you’re banged up, you need to let your coaches know.”

“I will, I promise.”

“And they want to know, believe me,” my dad adds. “The coaches will respect you more for telling them you’re hurt.”

“Got it.” I want to believe my dad, I really do, but it’s hard.

“Good.”

We eat our ice cream quietly for a few seconds. Then I say, "What about you, though, Dad? Did you ever take yourself out of a game when you were playing?"

He laughs. "You are definitely the funniest child I have."

"I'm the only child you have."

"Well, you're still the funniest," he says, winking. "It was a different time, Caleb. A very different time. No one asked to come out of a game, for any reason, unless you wanted to make sure you'd never go back in as long as you lived." He looks over at my mom. "Thank God that's all changed now, right, hon?"

As we drive home, I keep thinking about that.

That's all changed now.

Has it?

YOUTUBE VIDEO Sammy "Dinger" Springer, Amazing Touchdown Grab vs. Browns, 10.14.2002

ANNCR 1: . . . It's third and eight; the Jets have the ball at the Browns' twenty-two yard line . . . Two tight-end set . . . Evans drops back . . . Lewis picks up the linebacker blitz, giving Evans a chance to throw . . . He lofts it up toward the corner pylon . . . WHAT A CATCH! WHAT A CATCH BY SPRINGER! SAMMY SPRINGER WITH THE TOUCHDOWN GRAB, AND THE JETS GO UP 23–16 WITH ONLY TWO AND A HALF MINUTES LEFT ON THE CLOCK!

ANNCR 2: I can't believe he held on to that ball, Vince. The kid they call "Dinger" took one heckuva shot. The safety and the cornerback sandwiched him pretty good, one got him low, one got him high . . . Looked like possible helmet-to-helmet contact, too . . . Man, the refs are really letting 'em play out there . . . I tell ya, this kid Springer has really impressed me.

ANNCR 1: He might not be the fastest guy out there, or the quickest, but Sammy Springer has hands of glue, and he's as tough as they come.

ANNCR 2: He really is.

⁘⁘⁘

Sometimes when I can't sleep, I watch old videos of my dad.

And tonight, I can't sleep.

When I went upstairs after dinner to do homework, I put music on, like I always do. And that's when the headache came back. It's not as bad as before, but it's still there. A soft pounding behind my eyes, like someone playing drums with a sock.

I don't want to tell my mom or dad. So I tiptoe to the bathroom and gulp down a few Advil. Then I go back to my room and try to concentrate on my homework, but it's hard.

The light hurts. I turn it off.

The music is too loud. I turn it down.

I google "concussion aftereffects," but then close out of that window and shut my laptop before the search results come up.

I don't want to know.

10:18 PM
Nina
hey
hey
why did you leave so fast after the game
i don't know, i guess i was mad
at me?
at football
hahaha
i'm fine seriously
your head doesn't hurt at all?
maybe a little
i knew it
did you get any good pictures?
a few
what are you doing?
not much
watching some old videos to help me fall asleep
old videos of what
my dad

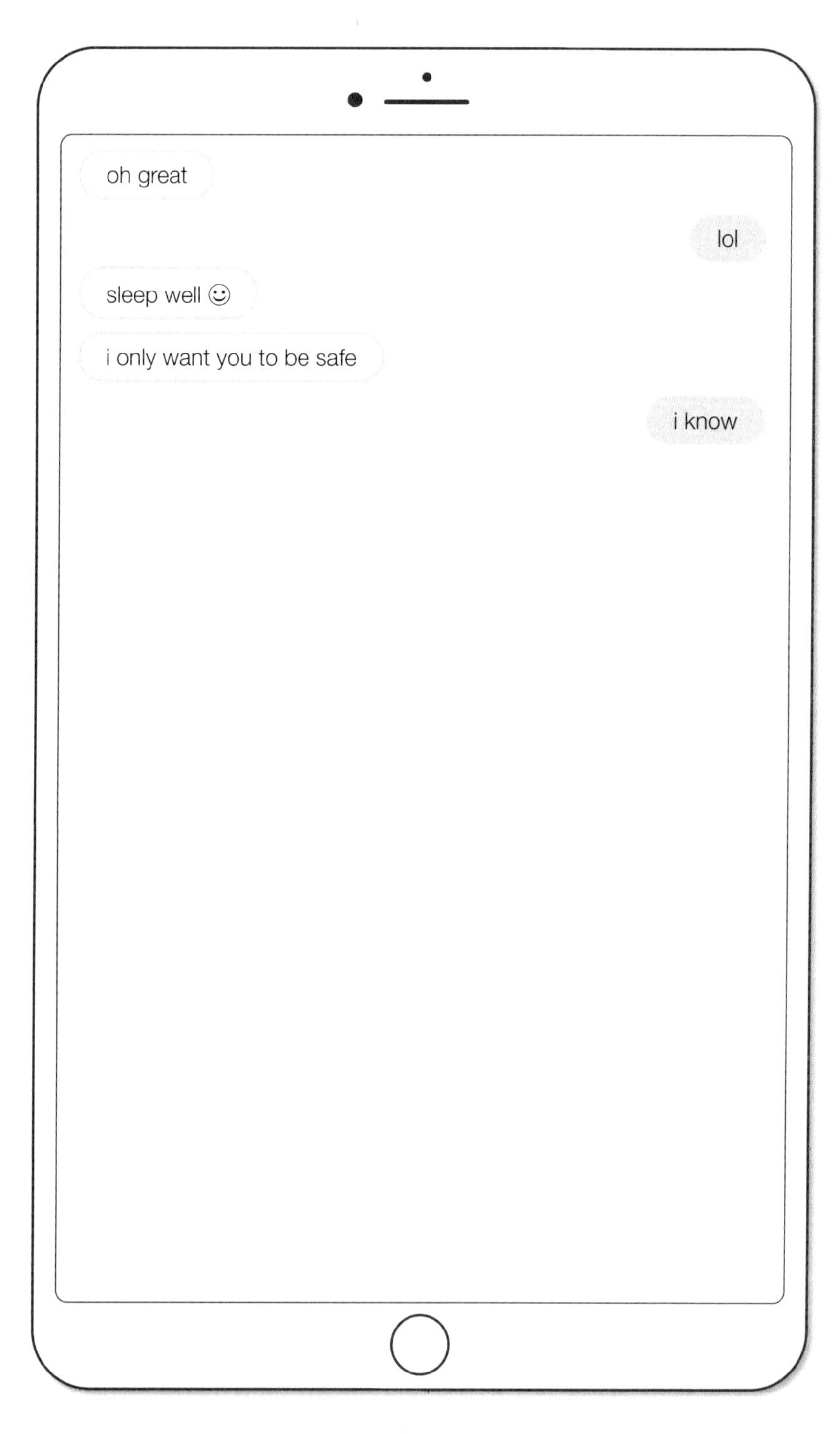
oh great
lol
sleep well ☺
i only want you to be safe
i know

The Advil starts to work. The throbbing becomes duller. I think maybe I can sleep. I lie down and close my eyes.

Five minutes go by.

Nothing.

I open the laptop back up.

If you search "Sammy Springer" or "Dinger Springer," a zillion hits come up. You have to narrow them down to get to the good stuff. So I search "Sammy Springer all-time best catches." I watch a bunch of clips I've seen before—from college and the pros. I'm always amazed at what a great pass-catcher my dad was. Anything near him, he caught. The focus, the hand strength, the perfect routes he ran—my dad had all the tools. If his career had lasted just a little longer, maybe he really would have made the Hall of Fame. But we'll never know.

I close out of "Sammy Springer all-time best catches" and think for a second. My head is still there, knocking softly, telling me it's not quite right. I think about trying to go to sleep. I decide not to. I search something else.

"Sammy Springer wild card."

The highlight of my dad's career was when he played in the 2005 Wild Card game. The Jets were playing the Chargers. He only had two catches for thirty-seven yards, but they were both so sweet. I've seen them more times than I can count. The first catch is the best.

⁂

YOUTUBE VIDEO
Twelve Yards the Hard Way, Wild Card Playoffs
1.8.2005

ANNCR 1: . . . Tight game early in the second quarter . . .

ANNCR 2: Jets are still trying to find their rhythm . . .

ANNCR 1: Pennington drops back, feeling the pressure . . . slings it out wide. Oh my! Somehow Sammy Springer comes up with that ball! A one-handed fingertip grab . . . Springer dances down the sidelines with two defenders draped all over him, finally gets dragged out of bounds after picking up the first down. What a play by Springer!

ANNCR 2: Could this be the spark the Jets needed? We'll see, but one thing is certain: When the team needs an energy play, an effort play, Sammy Springer delivers.

ANNCR 1: And he always has.

⁘⁘⁘

I know every second of this video by heart. I think it might be the video that made me become obsessed with football, and obsessed with playing in the NFL. My dad always says it's a combination of aggression and grace that makes the sport so mesmerizing, and he's right.

I watch the video five more times and then I finally fall asleep.

4

Up until two years ago, all I cared about was sports. Football in the fall, basketball in the winter, baseball in the spring. Posters of athletes on my bedroom walls.

Girls were the last thing on my mind.

Then, on the first day of seventh grade, this new girl walked through the door of my homeroom class.

I noticed her right away.

The first thing I noticed about her was that she didn't notice me.

She didn't care who I was. She didn't know that I was Caleb Springer. She didn't know that my dad was Sammy Springer.

That was cool.

I didn't talk to her for the first two months.

She sat in the front of the class with the kids who wanted to learn.

I sat in the back with the kids who wanted to goof off.

If you know anything about seventh grade, you know that those two groups of kids don't really hang out.

Then one day she came up to me in the hall while I was on my way to lunch.

"What is it about you?" she asked.

I looked at her.

I could make something up right now, and tell you that I said something funny and clever back, something like, "Uh, everything, I guess."

But the truth is, I froze.

Because even though I was Caleb Springer, and even though I was Sammy Springer's kid, the quarterback, that doesn't mean I'd ever actually talked to a real live human girl before.

Like I said, I hadn't been interested.

But all of a sudden, I was interested.

"Huh?"

Her eyes twinkled. "What is it about you?" she repeated.

"Wh-what do you mean?"

"I mean, all the other boys in the class seem to follow you around like little ducklings."

"Hahahahahaha." She was still waiting for me to say something else, though, so I went with "Huh?" again.

Real smooth, right?

"They obviously worship you," she said. "Like you're the king of the school or something."

By now, we were in the cafeteria. Heads were turning in our direction. Caleb Springer was talking to the new girl. This qualified as big news at Walthorne North Middle School.

"No, they don't," I said. "We're all, like, best friends. We hang out together."

She pointed, and I looked. Eric, Jamie, and a bunch of other guys were sitting at our usual table, looking up at me, waiting for me to take my usual seat.

All of a sudden, they reminded me of . . . well . . . little ducklings.

"Yo, Caleb!"

"Sit down awready!"

"What are you doing, bro?"

"Check out this video on Eric's phone!"

"Dude, let's go!"

The little ducklings were getting impatient.

I looked back at the new girl. "I gotta go."

"Quack, quack," she said. "I'm Nina."

⁘ ⁘ ⁘

Now here we are, the Monday after the Meadow Ridge game. I'm in the cafeteria again, but a few things have changed.

The first is, I gave up baseball and basketball. I had to. I mean, I love those sports, but in high school, football is a year-round thing. Training, conditioning, lifting, camps in the summer. You don't have a choice, especially if you're a quarterback.

Second, every day is like a big decision in terms of who I eat lunch with: my friends, who I've sat with pretty much every day since fourth grade, or my girlfriend, who I've sat with most days since about a month ago.

I walk into the seating area and see Eric and Jamie—they're at a table with a bunch of other guys, most of them on the freshman football team. They all look at me with hope in their eyes, and it's weird, I can't explain it, but there's something about that look that weirds me out a little. Maybe it's the pressure, or the expectations or something, I don't know. But I hesitate.

"You gonna sit, or what?" Eric half-asks, half-demands.

"Uh . . . actually I told Nina I'd get some homework done with her."

He nods without smiling. "Okay, yeah, cool."

Jamie squints up at me. "Since when do you do homework? Especially in the middle of the day?"

"He's a new man," Eric says.

They both laugh.

I don't.

⁂

"So, how are you feeling?" Nina asks as soon as I sit down. She's looking at me the way she does sometimes, the way that makes me feel like I'm a science project and she's the scientist.

"What do you mean?" I ask, even though I'm pretty sure I know what she means.

"Your head. How is it?"

"Oh yeah, uh, it's fine."

"How fine?"

"Totally fine."

She might not think I'm telling the truth, even though I am—my head doesn't hurt at all anymore. Over at the other table, Eric and Jamie have started balancing french fries on their noses. There is no way they would be asking me these questions right now. Or ever.

But Nina would, and is.

Which is one of the things I don't love about her.

And one of the things I love about her.

"Last night, you said it still hurt a little," she says.

"Yeah, it was just a headache and it was gone when I woke up."

Nina snorts with disgust. "Just a headache. Just a broken leg. Just a crushed pelvis or a separated shoulder or a sprained neck. And football's just a game, right?"

I laugh, which is what I always do when Nina goes on one of her anti-football rants.

She frowns, which is what she always does when I laugh after one of her anti-football rants.

"Seriously, I'm good," I tell her, hoping to end this conversation.

"Okay, fine," Nina says, deciding to let it go.

She takes a sip of her gross health juice. I sit back in my chair and stare up at the fluorescent lights in the ceiling.

"What?" Nina asks.

"What what?"

"What are you thinking about?"

I shrug. "I don't know . . . Sometimes I wish you liked football, even a tiny bit. You only see the bad stuff, or you only want to see the bad stuff, but it's so much more than that. It's, like, just so awesome."

" 'Just so awesome!' " she says, imitating me. Then she reaches across the table and squeezes my shoulder. "I like football *players*. Isn't that enough?"

Before I can respond to that with *absolutely* and *definitely*, a booming voice rings out. "SPRINGER!"

I turn around. Ron Johnson, our team captain, is approaching our table. He's trailed by some other kids on the team.

They kind of look like little ducklings—or, actually, large ducklings—but I'm not about to say that out loud.

Ron yells "SPRINGER!" again. By now, he's at our table. He pulls up a chair, flips it around backward, and sits down, right between Nina and me. The other guys stand around him in a semicircle.

"Excuse me, you're kind of, like, in my space," Nina says, but no one seems to care.

"What is UP!" Ron says. He has this way of speaking where he always puts extra emphasis on the last word he says. "Tell me EVERYTHING!"

"Uh . . . about what?"

"About the dude who came to the game with your DAD!"

"Oh, him. Yeah, he's an old friend of my dad's; they played together. He coaches up at State. I guess maybe he might want me to go there to play football."

Ron guffaws. "HA! That is freakin' NUTS!" He looks back at his friends, who all nod their agreement. "I mean, come on, man. You're a KID! You haven't done SQUAT!"

I try to laugh. "Ha! Yeah, no, I know."

Ron leans in and lowers his voice to practically a whisper. "You got one job, Springer, and that is to win football games for *this* team." It sounds more like a threat than a statement. "So don't you be thinking about playing any college ball. You focus on your JOB. Winning football games for Walthorne. That's IT."

"Of course, Ron, of course. I got it. You got nothing to worry about."

I can see Ron's body relax a little. "Okay, cool." Then he looks over at Nina and his eyes go wide, like he just realized she was there. "Whoa! We better let you get back to your little girlfriend. She's quite the HOTTIE!"

Nina rolls her eyes. "I've never been referred to as a 'hottie' before," she says. "I find it both rude and flattering. So stop it, and thank you."

Ron looks like he's just seen an alien, or a ninth-grade girl who had the nerve to give attitude to the captain of the varsity football team. "Uh, SORRY," he sputters. "No offense or anything, OKAY?"

Nina picks up her sandwich and takes a big bite. She chews slowly while everyone just watches and waits.

"Okay," she says, finally. "No offense taken."

Ron regains some of his status by jabbing a finger in my chest. "See you at PRACTICE. Get there early for extra stretching, CAPICHE?"

I give him a thumbs-up. "CAPICHE!"

Ron nods at his friends and they all walk away, mumbling to each other.

Nina shakes her head at me. "I was wrong before."

"Huh?"

"I like *one* football player."

WWHS
WALTHORNE HIGH SCHOOL RADIO
September 19

ALFIE:	Hey, everyone, it's me again, Alfie Jenks, associate sports editor, and you're listening to "Talking Sports." This is Alfie Jenks reporting.
RON:	You said that already.
ALFIE:	Said what?
RON:	Your name. You said it twice.
ALFIE:	Oh. Sorry.
RON:	I'm just razzin' you, bro. It's all good.
ALFIE:	"Bro"? I'm a girl.
RON:	So?
ALFIE:	Okay.
RON:	What grade are you in, anyway?

ALFIE: I'm a sophomore.

RON: So, like, how'd you get to be associate sports editor, and, like, call the games already, and stuff?

ALFIE: Because I take my job really seriously, I guess, and I'm pretty good at it.

RON: Cool. Respect, bro.

ALFIE: Right, thanks. I'm here with Ron Johnson, senior captain of the Walthorne High School Wildcats. Ron plays center on offense and noseguard on defense, and he's a two-year starter and was all-county last year. Ron, thanks for joining us.

RON: You got it.

ALFIE: So, Ron, the team is off to an undefeated start this season, with two easy wins. Tomorrow you're playing a pretty weak team in Comstock Prep. Can you tell our listeners what the game plan is?

RON: Of course not.

ALFIE: Uh, sorry, what?

RON: Of course I can't tell you our game plan, because then everyone would know. Including the guys over at Comstock. You're pretty good at your job, Alfie—you should know that.

ALFIE: Oh! [LAUGHS] Good point! So, uh, what are the keys to winning? Can you tell me that?

RON: Yeah sure, but it's not exactly rocket science. We need to score more. And we need to make sure they score less.

ALIFE: Got it.

RON: Happy to help.

ALFIE: Okay, well, thanks for—

RON: Dude, I'm messing with you!

ALFIE: "Dude"?

RON: To win, we gotta stop their running back, that kid Garrabino, I think his name is, and we got to protect our QB so he can make plays. Simple as that.

ALFIE: Yeah, he did take a pretty hard shot in the first game.

RON: Yeah, no kidding. Our coach let us know about that.

ALFIE: The QB we're talking about, of course, is rookie sensation Caleb Springer. Was the coach concerned that he was hurt?

RON: Nah, I don't think so. The kid said he was fine.

ALFIE: It's not supposed to be up to the player.

RON: I was there, he was fine. The coaches said he was fine, the trainers said he was fine.

ALFIE: Got it. Speaking of Caleb, what's it been like working a superstar freshman quarterback into the starting lineup? Any growing pains?

RON: Nope, no growing pains. Caleb is a great QB, for sure, and everyone is talking about him, I get it, but people need to realize it's not all about him, you know? We got, like, fifty kids on the roster, and no one player is any more important than anyone else. As the captain, I need to be sure we're all about the team, the players, and about winning and staying together. That's my job. So yeah, Caleb is a great player, but he's nothing without the rest of the guys. You feel me?

ALFIE: Yeah, absolutely, I feel you.

RON: Cool.

ALFIE: This has been "Talking Sports," with Alfie Jenks. I'd like to thank my guest, Captain Ron Johnson.

RON: Well, go ahead, then.

ALFIE: Go ahead what?

RON: Thank me.

ALFIE: Oh. Uh, thanks.

RON: You're welcome.

5

"Are you Sammy Springer?"

"Holy smokes, I know you."

"Hey, you're that guy! The football player! What's your name again?"

"Wait a second . . . No way! Hey, look, you guys, it's Dinger Springer!"

These are just a few of the phrases I've been hearing pretty much all my life whenever I'm out in public with my parents.

Mostly, it's really cool having a famous dad. All the things you might have heard are true—you get the best table at restaurants, maybe skip the line at an amusement park ride, your friends think you're cool, that kind of stuff. But it can get tiring. I know my mom gets sick of it sometimes. It's like she has to share my dad with the whole world.

Or, like on this particular occasion, she's sharing him with everyone at Stokeley's BBQ.

We go to Stokeley's the night before every game. It's a tradition that started three years ago. I'm usually pretty full from our team pasta dinner, so I only get a salad. My dad always gets the baby back ribs, my mom always gets the salmon, and my dad makes us share a macaroni and cheese. "Carb-load," he likes to say. "Best part of football."

Tonight, there's a steady stream of people who come up to us while we're eating. It's usually someone we don't know. They ask for an autograph or a picture. The men all want to shake my dad's hand.

"I used to watch you back in the day."

"Man, you were lightning quick."

"Can I get a picture? My dad is gonna love this."

We see a lot of people we know, too, but they don't bother us. They know better.

I'm amazed at how easily my dad deals with the fans. He's always friendly, making small talk, cracking jokes. And every time someone wants a picture, my dad grins like it's the most natural thing in the world.

The people walk away like they won the lottery.

"You're so good at being nice to people," I tell my dad.

"Watch and learn," he says. "Someday it's going to be you doing all this smiling and chatting."

"You think?"

"I know."

My mom glances at my dad. "That's enough talk about that. Let our son finish ninth grade first."

"Fair enough," says my dad. We all laugh. It feels good. Our team is off to a hot start and we feel like a playoff team.

While we wait for dessert to come—peach cobbler and key lime pie—my dad and I do what we always do.

We start talking about the next day's game.

This week we're playing Comstock Prep. They're never very good, and they lost big in their first two games. We're supposed to win by four or five touchdowns at least.

"Did you guys work on the two-minute drill?"

"Yeah, Dad. We covered it in practice."

"I noticed in the last game the play-calling was getting a little predictable."

"Dad, it's cool. We're playing Comstock."

"Doesn't matter. You need to be ready. Anything can happen. That's why they play the game."

I glance at my mom, who gives me a little eye roll. This is another part of our dinner tradition. My dad second-guessing everything our coach does. It would be even more annoying if my dad was ever wrong. But he never is.

He's about to ask me another question when a fan walks over to us—an older woman with white hair and a bright smile. My dad immediately jumps up to take her arm.

"I'm so sorry to interrupt," she says. "My name is Rose, and I just have to tell you, my husband and I enjoyed watching you play very much."

My dad gives her his A+ grin. "That is so sweet of you to stop by! What's your husband's name?"

"Oh, he's passed on," says the woman. "His name was Ed."

My dad gives the woman a hug, and you can see her melt into his arms a little bit. "I'm so sorry to hear that, Rose. I'm sure Ed was a great guy. Would you like a picture, maybe for your kids, or grandkids?"

She beams. "Oh yes, I'd like that very much."

My dad gives me a quick look, which is my cue to get up. "You're a sweet young man," Rose tells me as I take her phone. "What's your name?"

"Caleb," I say.

"Well, it's very nice to meet you, Caleb."

"Nice to meet you, too, ma'am."

My dad puts his arm around her. "It's people like you that make me glad I played the game, Rose." She smiles, and he smiles, and I take the picture.

When I give Rose her phone back, she says, "Your dad is a very fine man. I hope you grow up to be just like him."

"I do, too," I tell her.

My dad and I sit down, and it's back to business. "So, anyway, the game plan," he says. "What's the scheme? Are the coaches going to change up the offense?"

"What do you mean?" I ask.

"I mean, the pattern is always the same, Cae. First down, run. Second down, option. Third down with more than five yards to go, pass. Third down with less than five yards to go, another option. Any defensive coach who knows what he's doing is going to sniff that out real quick. You gotta mix things up and keep them off balance."

"Dad, are you serious? You want me to tell the coach he's predictable? Ha!"

He winks. "Well then, I might just do it."

"Go for it. And by 'go for it,' I mean please don't."

As we're laughing, another fan approaches the table. He's a man about my dad's age, maybe a little younger, and his eyes are wide. "Whoa, Sammy Springer! This is, like, this is totally awesome! I heard you lived around here, and now here you are!"

The guy seems like he's been drinking. My dad breaks out his friendly smile. "Hey, bud, how are ya?"

"Great!" The fan frowns. "Hey, like, whatever happened to you?"

My dad blinks a few times. "What do you mean?"

"I mean, like, I remember you were so good, you know? Like, an amazing receiver! And then, uh, you just kind of, like, disappeared."

"I didn't disappear. I retired after seven years in the league."

"Ohhhh." The guy looks like he's never heard the concept of retirement before. "But, like, why?"

"I was banged up," my dad explains patiently. "After a few years, my body wore down and it just wasn't worth it anymore."

"Bummer," the guy says. "So, like, you just quit?"

"Retired. There's a difference. Seven years is a good long career in the league." I can see my dad losing patience. "Now, if you don't mind, I'd love to finish my meal with my family."

"So wait, no picture?"

"Not right now. It was very nice to meet you."

The guy's face clouds over, like he just suffered the biggest disappointment of his life. His eyes turn angry. "Well, excuuuuse me, Mr. 'I wasn't tough enough for the NFL so I quit, but I'm still too good to take a picture with a fan.' Have a nice life."

The guy starts to walk away, then turns back for one final thought. "Oh, and you suck."

My dad shoots out of his chair and is inches from the guy's face in about one second flat. He still has his quickness, that's for sure. "What did you say?" My dad's voice is barely louder than a whisper, but it doesn't have to be. There's a look in his eyes that I've never seen before. Kind of like a cornered animal. "In front of my family? You want to say that again, friend?"

My dad isn't big by professional football standards, but he is big by normal human standards, and he's about two or three inches taller than this guy, who suddenly looks completely petrified.

"I—I, uh . . ."

My mom gets up and grabs my dad's arm. "Sammy. SAMMY! Honey, stop. It's not worth it. Sit down, please. Please."

My dad doesn't take his eyes off the guy. "Like I said, I'd like to finish my meal with my family. If you'll excuse me."

"Sure thing, buddy," the guy says, before scampering away. I realize the whole restaurant has quieted to a simmer. Everyone is waiting to see what my dad will do next. He slowly sits down. My mom sits, too.

"Anyway, where were we?" my dad says, completely normally. "Oh yeah. The team needs to add the element of surprise. You might want to try throwing more on first or second down."

I decide to follow his lead, and also pretend that the last forty-five seconds didn't happen. "So you want me to ask Coach Toffler about it?"

"Yeah, absolutely, run it by him if you can," my dad says. "But if you get an opportunity during the game to go for it, trust your gut—coaches never stay mad for long if you make the right call."

"Okay, Dad, sounds good. I'll do that."

I glance over at my mom. She smiles at me, but it's a nervous smile.

Dessert comes.

We eat quickly and quietly, then go home.

6

Walthorne High vs. Comstock Prep
Season Record: 2–0

They're better than we thought.

Or maybe we're tired. Or lazy, or uninterested. Or looking ahead to next week when we play New Medford, who's always one of the tougher teams in the league.

Maybe some of our seniors and juniors stayed up too late, playing video games or messing around online or doing other stuff.

Who knows the reason. But whatever it is, our game with Comstock Prep turns out to be a dogfight.

We're barely beating the worst team in the league.

People say that's one of the great things about sports—strange things happen all the time, and bad teams beat good teams, and sometimes even terrible teams beat great teams.

But it doesn't feel like one of the great things about sports today.

At halftime we're up 14–6. Coach Toffler lights into us. He screams for ten minutes straight, saying we're a disgrace, an embarrassment, we're horrible, our grandfathers could play better than us, we suck, and a lot worse swear words than that.

No one moves a muscle. Not even the assistant coaches.

For a while I listen to every word the coach says. Then when he starts repeating himself for the fourth time about how terrible we're playing, my mind starts to wander.

I think about random stuff.

I think about the drunk fan at the restaurant, and how my dad almost knocked him into the next county.

I think about our two-minute drill, and how we might actually need it today.

I think about how hard and how long the coach is screaming at us. I wonder if piano teachers yell at their students this way. Or drama teachers. Or scout leaders, or math tutors.

If they did, they'd probably be arrested.

If a parent yelled at their kids like that, someone would call child protective services.

But Coach Toffler is still hollering.

I take a quick peek at Ron, the captain. He's staring at the ground, but I'm pretty sure I see a slight smile on his face.

I can't blame him. It is kind of funny.

"AND YOU!" screams the coach. "ARE YOU KIDDING ME RIGHT NOW??"

It takes me about ten seconds to realize who he's screaming at.

Me.

"Sor— Uh, Coach?"

But he's just getting warmed up.

"WHAT ARE YOU SMIRKING AT?!? YOU THINK THIS IS SOME SORT OF JOKE? AM I A STAND-UP COMEDIAN UP HERE FOR YOUR AMUSEMENT? DAMN IT, SPRINGER, GET YOUR HEAD OUT OF YOUR ASS AND INTO THE FOOTBALL GAME!"

"Yes, sir!"

I think coaches think they're helping players when they scream and go nuts. I think they think it gets us fired up, like if they get really mad, we'll get really mad, too, and then we'll go out there and run wild over the other team.

But I don't think it works that way.

I think when coaches scream at kids, it makes the nervous kids more nervous. And it makes the confident kids like me get irritated and distracted. And any athlete will tell you, it's pretty much impossible to do your best when you're nervous or irritated or distracted. Your body doesn't work as well. Your mind loses focus. Everything gets messed up.

So of course we come out in the third quarter and lay a total egg. Comstock runs the opening kickoff back to our forty-two yard line and scores four plays later. They make the two-point conversion and it's a tie game. Then, on our first offensive play, I try to hand off the ball to Mitch Sellers, and he drops it. Or, I drop it. Either way, the ball is loose. FUMBLE! Luckily, Ron falls on it, so we keep the ball.

Ron isn't smiling anymore. He comes back to the huddle with murder in his eyes. He says about twenty words, fifteen of which are swears. The other five are, "SO GET IT TOGETHER! NOW!"

But we don't get it together. It stays apart.

The score is 14–14 as we head into the fourth quarter. Our defense is handling things pretty well on their end, but the offense is just not stepping up. It's like what my dad said at dinner: We're too predictable, and the Comstock defense knows what we're going to do before we do it.

I think about his advice. *You gotta mix things up and keep them off balance.*

We get the ball back on our own forty-six yard line with around four minutes to go.

On first down, I hand off to Henry Kosky, the fullback, and he gets stuffed for a one-yard gain.

On second down, I pitch the ball to Mitch Sellers on an option, and he scratches out maybe two yards.

On third down, I drop back to pass, but no one is open, of course—Comstock knows exactly what we're doing. I'm about to be sacked for a loss, but I manage to wriggle away from two defenders and scramble for nine yards.

First down.

Ron Johnson gives me a glare, but I can see a little respect poking through. "Way to toughen up, PRETTY BOY!"

My legs feel a little lighter and my head feels a little clearer.

One of our receivers, Brett Rose, checks in with the play we're supposed to run. OT Slant Left High Lightning. Which is just a complicated way of saying I'm supposed to hand the ball to Henry Kosky for a run off the left side. Again.

We huddle up. I start to tell everyone the play. Then I stop. "Guys," I say. "We're going to try something different. Coach sent in OT Slant Left High Lightning. But I'm going to fake the handoff to Henry. Brett, act like you're gonna block your guy the way you always do on a run play, then take off down the sideline. If you're open, I'll hit you. Otherwise, I'll just throw the ball away."

I stop talking and look up. Ten guys are staring me in the face.

"Wait, WHAT?" says Ron. "What are you talking about? You don't want to run the play that Coach sent in?"

"I just think this might work better. We've run every time on first down. They're not expecting a pass."

Everyone waits as Ron decides what to do. Finally, he nods. "Okay. Let's do it." He pokes me in the chest. "You better know what you're doing."

The guys nod. Ron is the captain—what he says goes. We break the huddle. The Comstock defense lines up. I can tell by their formation they're playing the run.

"HUT!"

I veer toward Henry with the ball outstretched. He cradles his arms like he's about to receive the ball. I hold it out to him, then pull it back at the last second. Henry plunges into the line and gets swarmed on by the defense. Meanwhile, I roll out to my right and spot Brett streaking down the sideline.

One move past his guy, and he's wide open.

I heave the ball as far as I can throw it, which is about fifty yards. Brett catches it in full stride and sprints untouched into the end zone.

TOUCHDOWN, BABY.

⁘ ⁘ ⁘

WWHS
WALTHORNE HIGH SCHOOL RADIO
TRANSCRIPT OF PLAY-BY-PLAY
ALFIE JENKS AND JULIAN HESS

ALFIE: Wow, what a call! Caleb Springer completely crossed up the entire defense right there with that brilliant fake! Walthorne finally takes the lead on these committed Commandos from Comstock!

JULIAN: Haha! That's a lot of "com" words, Alfie! I like it! COMgratulations!

ALFIE: Credit goes to Coach Toffler there, for sure. The team could use more of that kind of creative play-calling as the season goes on, especially when they start facing the harder teams.

JULIAN: Harder schmarder, Alfie. We're gonna whup all these guys.

ALFIE: I thought we talked about this, Julian. Please try to be a little more professional while calling games.

JULIAN: But my Twitter followers love the jokes!

ALFIE: Ugh.

⁘⁘⁘

The rest of us sprint into the end zone and mob Brett. We're screaming at the top of our lungs. Ron lifts me in the air. "YEAH, BABY! PHENOM BOY GETS IT DONE!"

We run back to the sideline. Coach Toffler comes out and puts his hand on my arm to stop me. He's not smiling.

"What was that about?" he asks.

I take Buck off and catch my breath. The rest of the team is celebrating on the sideline, and boy, would I love to join them.

He asks again. "I said, what was that about?"

I feel someone next to me, and glance over. It's Ron. "What's up, Coach?" he says.

"I'm talking to Caleb."

"Cool." Ron looks at me and nods. "Nice play." He jogs away to join the other players.

Coach hasn't taken his eyes off me. "Do you want to answer my question?"

"Uh, sure, yes, sir. We had the play called, you know, Slant Left High Lightning, but I saw something in the way the defense was lined up and so I changed the play. I thought it might be open, and, uh, it was."

"What's our policy about that?"

"Huh?"

"What's our policy about play-calling?"

“Uh, the plays come from the sidelines.”

“How many?”

“Sorry?”

“How many plays?”

“All of them.”

“That’s right.”

“I’m sorry, Coach.”

The coach stares me down for ten more seconds—which feel like ten minutes—then smacks my shoulder pad, hard.

“Smart play. Real smart play. This week in practice we’ll talk about giving you some more play-calling responsibilities.”

“Yes, sir, Coach. Thank you, Coach.”

His lips twitch. “But you’re benched for the rest of the game.”

⁘ ⁘ ⁘

Comstock sags after the touchdown. They fumble the kickoff, so we get the ball back. My replacement is a senior named Arch Daniels. He started as a junior, so he wasn’t too happy when I came along. But he’s a nice kid and he’s been pretty decent about it. The coach doesn’t let Arch throw the ball at all, though—he just hands off four times to run out the clock. We win 21–14.

In the locker room, I find Ron and thank him for having my back. He grunts, not wanting to give me too much.

The coach gives the game ball to Brett Rose.

"This is for catching that pass," he tells Brett. "Because if you'd dropped it, none of you would have ever seen Caleb Springer again."

7

When I first started playing sports, my dad told me three things:

1) Never act better than anyone else
2) Never taunt a losing opponent when you win
3) Never blame anybody else when you lose

Being an athlete means being a sportsman, he would say. *And sportsmen behave with dignity.*

I learned my lesson well, but growing up, I slipped a few times. I remember one time in particular, when I was in sixth grade. We'd just won the league championship, and after the game, a bunch of us went to Dusty's. There were some kids from the team we'd beaten, sitting there with their families. As soon as we saw them, someone on our team started singing "We Are the Champions," that song that everyone sings when they win a championship, and so of course the rest of the guys joined in, including me. Everyone thought it was funny—even the players from the other team smiled. No one thought anything of it. But as soon as we got in the car, my dad turned around and glared at me. I could tell from the look on his face that I wasn't going to enjoy the next few minutes.

If I ever see you do anything like that again, you will be grounded for a year.

I'm happy to report that I've never been grounded for a year.

⁂

But that doesn't mean I'm perfect, either.

After the Comstock game, the sideline is crowded. I look for Nina but then remember she's with her parents, visiting her big sister at college.

My friends rush up to me, smacking me on the back. Eric hollers in my face. Jamie punches me in the shoulder. Little kids wearing their travel football jerseys look at me like I'm a god. Older girls smile at me.

Behave with dignity.

I hear my dad's voice in my head, but sometimes it's softer than other times. And right now it's really soft.

As I'm celebrating with Eric and Jamie, I holler, "YEAH, BABY!" and start jumping up and down. "THAT WAS MY CALL! THAT WAS ALL ME, BOYS!"

"What do you mean?" Eric asks.

"I CALLED THAT PLAY!" I know I sound full of myself, but I'm too excited to care. "The coach wanted to run the usual BS running play and I was like, no way, man! I'm throwing the deep ball! I told the guys in the huddle and Ron was like, are you serious, and I was like, you're damn right! And he was like, okay, and, well, the rest is history!"

"Whoa, the coach was cool with that?" Eric asks, but I don't feel like answering.

Jamie is about to say something when a couple of the varsity defensive linemen come over and pound me on the back. They start firing questions at me, like asking me if I want to go get beers (I say "Uh . . .") and where my girlfriend is (I say "Uh . . ." again), and one of them, a big dude named Nathan, makes a dumb joke, and I laugh hard, and then we're all laughing, and by the time I remember that I was talking to Eric and Jamie, they're gone. I tell myself to text them later, even though I know I'll forget.

After a few more minutes of acting like little kids with some of the biggest kids you'll ever see, I find my parents. My mom gives me a big hug, as usual. "Thank God you're okay."

"I'm great, Ma."

"No bells rung?"

"No bells rung."

My dad half-smiles when he sees me coming, and we do the handshake thing. "You guys had your hands full out there today," he says.

I grunt out a laugh. "Yeah. I guess we just, like, thought we were going to kill them or something."

"You took them too lightly. Lucky it didn't cost you."

"Yeah. I know."

"Can't let that happen, Caleb, ever. No game is a gimme. Keep it in mind for next time."

"I will."

I wait a few seconds, because I don't want there to be any negative energy in the air when I bring up my next topic. "But, uh, Dad? Did you see what happened at the end of the game?"

"You mean your touchdown pass? Of course I saw. The coach made a good play call there, finally. And you made a great throw."

I try not to smile. "Coach didn't call that play, Dad. I did."

"*You* did?" My dad frowns. "What do you mean, *you* did?"

"It means I took your advice, Dad. We were getting too predictable, just like you said. Their defense knew what was coming. So I changed the call in the huddle, from a first-down run to a pass. And it worked like a dream!"

"My advice?"

"Yeah, Dad. From dinner last night. We talked about this exact thing, remember?"

My dad stares at the ground for a second, then he glances over at my mom. "I, uh . . . uh . . . honey?"

She doesn't hear him, though, because she's talking to another mother.

"Honey, can you come here a sec?" my dad says, louder. He has a strange look on his face, almost desperate. "HONEY? HONEY???"

My mom hears that last one. She jerks her head around. "What, Sammy? What is it?"

My dad suddenly looks embarrassed. "I, uh . . . Caleb and I were just talking about our great conversation at dinner last night, and how it helped him in the game today."

"Oh, sure," my mom says, nodding. "You mean about how the offense was getting predictable, how they needed to mix up the play-calling more? You said Caleb should change a call in the huddle if he had to, even without asking the coach, because coaches never stay mad for long if you win. Remember, honey?"

She reminds me of one of those lawyers on TV who's trying to get the witness to say something.

My dad smiles. "Oh yeah . . . yeah, of course I do. Sure!"

I try to be helpful. "It was right after that drunk guy asked you for a picture, remember, Dad?"

"Absolutely!" My dad is nodding vigorously. "He was a terrific guy. I mean, a little drunk, like you said, but a great fan. I love all my fans!"

I feel a weird buzzing in my head.

"No, Dad," I say quietly. "The guy was a jerk. He called you a quitter. You almost ripped his head off."

Again, he looks at my mom. "That's right, he was a jerk," she tells him. "You remember, right, honey?"

"Right! Of course I remember." But my dad isn't nodding this time. This time, he's staring up into the sky, as if searching for a distant memory.

A distant memory of something that happened last night.

I look at my mom. She looks at me. I think I see a tear in her eye. My dad keeps his eyes on the sky, staring and searching.

But the only things he finds up there are clouds.

PART II
Storm

8

Nina is in a band.

They're called Fluffy Pillow. I don't know why. When I asked her what that meant, she said bands don't have to explain the meaning of their names.

Fluffy Pillow plays a lot of music from before I was born. According to Nina, the best music ever made was recorded between 1964 and 1981. She talks about that a lot. I like music, too, of course, but not like Nina—it's one of the two most important things to her. The other one is photography.

My two most important things are football and, uh, I guess talking about football.

The day after the Comstock game, I'm sitting at dinner with my parents. The last twenty-four hours haven't been great, to be honest. No one has really talked about what happened after the game. My dad's been acting like it wasn't that weird that he forgot about our conversation. Who knows, maybe he's right. My mom said something to me about Dad being "under a lot of stress and distracted by work stuff," and that was about it. I'm smart enough not to ask any more questions. My dad would probably get mad. I might bring it up with my mom at some point. I mean, I want to, but I don't want to.

At dinner we talk about boring stuff for a while. Then my dad says, "So, are you excited about the road trip next week?"

At first I'm confused, because we have a home game next week. It takes me a few seconds to realize he's talking about the trip we're taking up to State, to watch the college game with my dad's friend Brandon.

"Oh yeah, absolutely!"

My dad smiles and takes a sip of his beer. "Everything's arranged. Great seats, tour of the field, even a visit to the locker room after the game. I set it all up."

"Wow, that's awesome! Thanks, Dad."

My mom makes a goofy sad face. "I don't want to think about you leaving for college," she says. "Ever."

I laugh, while my dad squeezes her arm. It's a nice, relaxed moment, so I figure it's a good time to bring something up. "Nina has a gig tonight at Grandage Hall. Is it okay if I go?"

My dad raises his eyebrows. "A gig?"

“It’s a word that musicians use. It means ‘performance.’ ”

“Jeez, I’m slow, but I’m not *that* slow,” my dad says, laughing. “I know what it means. What’s Grandage Hall?”

I hesitate. From what I’ve heard, Grandage Hall is like a bar for high school kids. There’s no alcohol, of course, but it can still get rowdy. And needless to say, my dad is pretty strict about that stuff. Especially during football season.

I end up going with, “Just some place where kids hang out.”

“Sounds like a lot of fun, Caleb,” my mom says. She looks at my dad. “Don’t you think so, honey?”

“How late does this ‘gig’ go?” my dad asks.

“I’m not sure.”

“Well, we work out every Sunday morning, first thing. I don’t like to mess with the routine.”

I knew this was coming, so I’m prepared. “I thought about that. I’ll be ready. Maybe just this once we can start an hour later?”

“I swim at nine on Sundays, Cae, you know that.” He’s trying to be nice—I can tell by his use of my nickname, but I’m still pretty sure where this is going to end up.

“I’ll be ready. You gotta trust me, Dad, come on.”

"Come on? Come on?" My dad drops his napkin on his plate, gets up, and starts walking in circles around the kitchen table. "Don't you understand what I'm trying to do, Caleb? I'm trying to help you. I'm trying to teach you what it means to work. To go after something. To become the best. Fate already did the hard part for you. You were born with a rare talent. Now all you have to do is work. Work! Every day, the same routine, no days off, so it becomes as much a part of your life as breathing. You wake up every morning and say to yourself, 'Today I'm going to do everything I can to be the best.' And then the next day and the day after that and the day after that, you'll wake up and you'll BE the best. But if you break that routine, just once, that's all it takes. Because if you break it once, it's easier to break it again. And again. And again and again and again. And soon, the work stops. And the purpose stops. And everything stops. And it's over! Your dream is over! Your LIFE is OVER!" He pauses, and I notice he's breathing a little hard. "But, hey. If you want to throw it away to go see your girlfriend do a 'gig,' then be my guest. Just don't come crying to me when you're wondering where it all went wrong."

He stops talking, and all of a sudden it's silent. A fly lands on the lamp near the door, walks around in a circle for five seconds, then buzzes away.

My mom sips her water. "Be that as it may," she says, quietly but firmly, "I don't see the problem with Caleb going to the concert, as long as he promises to get a good night's sleep so he can be ready for tomorrow's workout. Does that make sense to you, Caleb?"

"Absolutely. Thanks, Mom."

"Of course, honey."

My dad blinks a few times, like he just woke up. He sighs, and the air goes out of his body.

"Okay. I'm sorry. Maybe I'm being too rigid. It's possible that a little fun might be just what the doctor ordered around here."

I don't look at my dad. I don't even move. I don't want to do anything to change his mind.

"What instrument does Nina play?" he asks.

"Bass. I've seen videos of her. She's really good."

"What kind of music?"

"Old music. Like, classic rock."

"My kind of music." He smiles. "Have a great time, okay? We'll work out in the morning, and if for some reason you're too tired, we'll figure something out for the afternoon."

"Sounds good, Dad."

"Well, I've got to go do some paperwork. I'll be in the study if anyone needs me."

My dad kisses my mom's shoulder and walks out of the room.

My mom closes her eyes for a few seconds, then opens them. She stares straight ahead as she speaks. "I know."

I tell myself I don't know what she's talking about. "What do you mean, Ma?"

She looks at me and smiles, but her eyes are sad.

"Go enjoy the concert," she says.

9

Grandage Hall is rocking when I walk in.

The first thing I notice is a blast of sound. Music, of course, and also shouting. Everyone is trying to be heard over the music. But the music wins every time.

The second thing I notice is the darkness. I can't see anything or anyone except the musicians. After about two minutes, I can make out shapes. But no faces.

The third thing I notice is a really wet floor. I slip for a second, and an image pops into my mind of my dad standing over my hospital bed, saying, *You're out for the season because someone spilled SODA on the FLOOR?* I make sure to take very small steps.

The fourth thing I notice is my brain telling me, *You're definitely not in middle school anymore.*

Nina is onstage with her band, playing a song I don't know. I wave to her, but there's no possible way she sees me. A bunch of people are dancing. It takes me a minute to realize they're all girls. The boys are standing around, watching the girls dance. No, wait. There's one boy dancing. But he's just by himself, twirling around in a circle. I'm not even sure you can technically call it dancing. But it seems like he's having a really good time.

I look around for familiar faces, but can't find any. A feeling bubbles up in my stomach and I'm not sure what it is at first. Then I know. It's insecurity. Which is weird, because I've never really felt it before. But now I know what it's like to stand there by yourself while no one even notices you.

It doesn't feel great, to be honest.

"SPRINGER!"

I hear the booming foghorn of Ron Johnson. Usually that voice makes me nervous, but tonight it's the sweetest sound I've ever heard.

There's a painful smack on my back. "Boy Wonder is allowed to come out and PLAY?"

I ignore that dig. "Hey, Ron, what's going on? Um, have you seen, like, any of the guys?"

Ron laughs, and some sort of liquid leaks out of his mouth. I think it might be beer, which is weird, since there's definitely no beer allowed in here. "The guys? You mean the freshmen NIMRODS?"

"Uh, okay, yeah, I guess." I decide to change the subject, and point up to the stage. "Hey, they sound pretty good."

Ron peers up at the stage. "Yeah, whatever, I barely know any of these songs." He squints harder. "Hey, is—isn't that, like, your girlfriend up there?"

"I guess, yeah. Nina. You met her at lunch."

Ron nods approvingly. "What is she, like, some hot chick guitar player?"

"Bass, actually."

"That's what I'm TALKING about!" Ron frowns, like he suddenly realizes he's talking to a freshman. "So listen," he says, "I gotta go. Hope you find your buddies." He smacks me again, this time on my non-throwing shoulder. "DON'T BREAK CURFEW OR YOUR DAD IS GONNA SEND YOU AWAY TO MILITARY SCHOOL!"

I rub my shoulder. *That freakin' hurt.*

I carefully walk over to where they're serving the soda that everyone is slipping on. Right when I get there, someone jumps on my back.

"YO, DUDE!"

It turns out it's three someones—Eric, Jamie, and Kenny. I'm thrilled to see them. We smack one another around and high-five and for a minute it feels like we're little kids pretending to be in high school. Then I remember that no, we actually ARE in high school.

"THE BAND IS REALLY GOOD!" Eric shouts.

"YEAH!" I shout back. "I DON'T KNOW TOO MANY OF THESE SONGS, THOUGH."

Eric shakes his head and screams, "ME NEITHER." That's when we realize that there's no point in trying to have an actual conversation while the band is playing, so we just nod along to the music. It's a little ridiculous, but it's a lot better than doing it alone.

I see Ron and his friends out of the corner of my eye. It's pretty much all the seniors on the football team, and they're waving their hands in the air and shouting something I can't hear. Other kids are staring at them, with a look in their eyes that says, *You guys are so obnoxious, but I still wish I could be a part of it.*

The song ends. The lead singer, some guy I don't know, waits for the cheers to end and then speaks into the microphone. "Thanks, everybody! We're Fluffy Pillow, and we're really excited to be playing for you tonight. So, usually we play old songs that my parents and your parents love, but right now we're going to change it up and play an original song, written by our bass player, Nina Rojas."

The crowd murmurs. I feel my ears start to get hot. I had no idea Nina wrote songs, especially a song that she was going to play in front of pretty much the whole school. For a second I get mad at her for not telling me she wrote songs. Then I get mad at myself for never asking if she wrote songs. Then I get nervous that the song might be terrible, and I would be embarrassed. Then I get mad at myself again for worrying about my own embarrassment if the song is bad, instead of supporting Nina.

This whole thing takes about four seconds.

Nina steps up to the microphone. She looks nervous, or maybe just shy, which are two things she normally is not.

"This song is called 'The Only Place,'" she says, barely audible.

The crowd hushes as the song begins. It starts soft.

Nina sings:

I couldn't be further from you

You couldn't be further from me

But right next to each other

Is the only place we wanna be

You spend time doing this

I spend time doing that

But doing separate things together

Is the only place we wanna be at

I feel my entire body start to tighten up as I realize the song is about us.

Heads are turning in my direction. Or maybe I'm just imagining it. Hard to know for sure, since I'm standing there, frozen, staring at the stage.

They say opposites attract

I guess maybe that's true

But I don't want to subtract

Me from you

You're always hot, I'm always cold

You like the sun, I like the rain

But, really, who cares about the weather

Because the only thing we agree on

Is the only thing that matters

And the only place we want to be

Is together

As the band keeps playing, I feel an elephant jump on my back. But it's not an elephant, obviously—it's Ron. "*DUDE! WHAT THE EFF!*"

Right behind him is half the varsity team, all screaming, shouting, and yelling pretty much the same thing: "YOUR GIRLFRIEND IS SINGING A SONG ABOUT YOU! YOU MUST BE FREAKING OUT RIGHT NOW!!!"

I'm not about to try to answer them. Even though they're giving me a hard time, part of them must think it's cool. Because that's what I think. Part of me is totally embarrassed, and part of me thinks it's totally cool.

I look up at Nina, and she's looking right at me. She's smiling, and then she winks. It's like she's telling me, *Sorry, dude, but this is what you signed up for. Take it or leave it.*

I want to take it.

The band turns it up a notch. They're so loud now that even Ron Johnson can't compete with them.

Nina sings:

It's not about you

And it's not about me

It's about us

It's about trust

It's about knowing we don't always have to agree

We're the whole, not the parts

One soul from two hearts

We're tied together, and we're free

And right next to you

Is the only place I wanna be

The song ends. There's like a second or two of silence, like everyone is trying to absorb what they just heard, and then the place explodes in yells, whoops, and whistles.

"We're gonna take a quick break—back in a few," the lead singer says, but it's hard to hear him over the cheering.

The band bows, and Nina is grinning from ear to ear.

My friends surround me, telling me how awesome that was. The seniors are there, too, pounding me on the back—I guess they decided that it's okay to have a girl sing you a song in public.

Eric is the only one who hangs back. I make my way through the backslappers and walk over to him. He smiles and nods slowly. "She's really talented," he says.

"Yeah, I guess so."

"Did you know about that song?"

"No way, dude! That was a total surprise."

"Cool."

I try to think of something else to say, but I can't. And I really want to go find Nina and congratulate her.

"So, yeah . . . I should . . ."

Eric manages a real smile. "Oh yeah, of course, man, go ahead. Tell her I thought the song was awesome. Seriously. She was great."

"I will."

I fist-bump Eric and slip out of the crowd before anybody else notices. It's almost like I'm leaving him behind, literally. It makes me feel bad.

Nina looks happier than I've ever seen her. She's surrounded by a bunch of people I don't know, probably photography friends and musicians and those kinds of people. She reminds me of someone, but I can't quite figure it out at first. Then it hits me.

She reminds me of me, after a football game.

When Nina spots me, she hugs three people, kisses two others on both cheeks, then runs over. Her eyes are shining and her smile is everything.

We hug, and the words rush out of her like a waterfall. "How was it? Was it okay? Are you mad that I didn't tell you about that song? Were you embarrassed? I'm really sorry if you were. I just didn't know how to tell you and I guess I kind of wanted it to be a surprise. Was that dumb? Are you mad? No, seriously, are you mad?"

I laugh. "Well, to be honest, I was a little surprised at first, and my friends were, like, ragging on me, but then the song was so awesome that we were all just, you know, like, super impressed."

She looks at me like she can't quite believe what I'm saying. "Wait, so you really liked the song?"

“Was it about us?” I ask her.

She smacks me on the arm. “Boy, football is starting to mess up your head for real! Of course it was about us, you dummy.”

“Oh. Well, actually I didn’t like the song.”

Her face clouds over.

“I loved the song.”

She squeals and jumps and then she kisses me. On the mouth.

I kiss her back. On the mouth.

We keep kissing.

It takes me a few seconds to realize two things.

One, everyone is staring at us.

And two, we’ve never done that in public before.

10

It isn't until we're at Jensen's, the diner where everyone hangs out, that I have the nerve to ask Nina about the thing we've both been thinking about since the second it happened.

"So, uh . . ."

Well, I thought I had the nerve. Turns out, not quite.

She grins. "So, uh . . . what?"

"You know."

"No, I don't know."

I look at her, but she shakes her head. She's going to make me say it.

So I do, finally.

"Everyone saw us kiss."

"So?"

Good question. "Uh, well, you know . . . Did it . . . uh . . . I guess that means that the world knows we're kind of officially girlfriend and boyfriend, right?"

She laughs, seemingly satisfied that she's made me suffer enough. "I'm cool with it if you're cool with it."

"I'm cool with it."

We let that hang there for a few seconds as we both check our phones for absolutely no reason.

"Are your friends cool with it?" she asks me, out of the blue.

"What? I mean . . . yeah, of course, why wouldn't they be?"

"I don't know." Nina eats a fry while I wait for her to say more. "I guess maybe it's, like, they don't seem to like me very much."

"They like you as much as they would any girlfriend I had, to be honest."

"What do you mean?" Nina asks. "They're jealous?"

"I guess." I hesitate for a second before continuing, because I know what I'm about to say isn't going to make me sound all that great. But I say it anyway. "It's not just you, though, you know? It's a bunch of things, like the fact that I'm the starting quarterback on varsity, and I'm getting all this attention and stuff. But also, I'm not sure what they want from me sometimes. Like, if I have the talent and I put in the work, is that supposed to make me feel bad?"

"Of course not," Nina says.

“What about you?” I ask. “Are your friends upset because you play in a band and wrote a great song about your *boyfriend*?”

“No,” she says, quietly. “They’re really happy for me.”

“That’s lucky,” I say.

The conversation has broken our celebratory mood a little bit. We deal with it by checking our phones again, and then the lead singer from her band comes over and gives her a big hug from behind.

“GREAT SHOW!” the guy says. “You were on fire tonight!”

“So were you!” Nina tells him. “That was our best gig ever, by far.”

“Well, we’ve only had two, but yeah, totally!”

They look at each other with such excitement and happiness and pride that I suddenly feel a ridiculous twinge of jealousy myself.

The singer goes off to hug someone else, and I exhale. “What’s his name again?” I ask Nina.

“Oh man, I should have introduced you. I’m sorry! That’s Brian.”

“He’s really good.”

“Yeah, he’s amazing.”

"How long have you two known each other?"

Nina lets out a quick giggle. "He's gay."

"Oh. So?"

"So you've got nothing to worry about there."

It's my turn to laugh. "That's, like, the last thing I was worried about!"

Nina's eyes twinkle when she smiles. "If you say so."

My phone buzzes. It's a text from my dad. Two words:

when home?

I quickly turn my phone over on the table.

"Who's that?" asks Nina.

"My dad."

The phone buzzes again.

it's getting late, you need to come home

This time I put the phone in my pocket.

Nina's smile fades. "You look stressed all of a sudden. What's going on?"

"I don't really want to get into it."

"Oh okay," Nina says, but I can tell by the change in her voice that it's pretty much the opposite of okay.

I look everywhere but at her.

"You can't be like that with me," she says. "Not if we're going to try to make this, you know, an actual thing."

I exhale heavily. "I don't know what you're—"

"Yes, you do," she says, before I can finish my lie.

The drummer from the band comes over, but before she can say anything, Nina says, "Not right now, Becca, sorry."

"Oh okay, cool," Becca says, and walks away.

Nina watches me and waits.

"I think something might be up with my dad," I say.

I'm not exactly sure what I'm thinking, but whatever it is, it's the first time I've said it out loud.

Her face softens. "What kind of something?"

"Something like, with his behavior. Like, with—he's—"

I stop talking, because I realize I'm not sure how to end that sentence. She leans in, and the noise and crowd and chaos in the diner start to fade away, like the end of a song. But Nina doesn't say anything. She just waits for me to be ready to say more.

"He's just gotten a lot more intense lately," I add. "A little . . . weird. And forgetful, sometimes. My mom thinks so, too."

Nina's eyes narrow. "Is this a football thing? Like, because of an injury or something?"

I feel the blood in my body get hot. "Why would you think that?"

"I don't know. I feel like I read something somewhere about—"

"No, of course not!" I say, cutting her off. "He's, like, forty-six years old! He's just, like, he's stressing out because I'm in high school now and starting on varsity and there's a lot more pressure, and he just really wants to make sure I take advantage of my talent, and so he's, like, acting a little freaked out because of it."

"Okay, okay," Nina says. "If you say so."

"I know so."

I'm not sure Nina's going to leave it at that—she rarely does—but before we can go any further, Hurricane Ron blows in. "THERE THEY ARE!!!!"

That's followed by the unmistakable sound of a bunch of kids stampeding toward me.

When Ron reaches our table, he immediately puts me in a headlock. "DUDE! You never told us that your girlfriend was a ROCK STAR!"

I'm struggling to breathe, so Nina answers for me. "I'm hardly a rock star. I just like playing music."

Ron decides that a live quarterback is better than a dead one, so he eases up on the choke hold. The kids behind him take little shots at me—slaps, ear twists, noogies, that sort of thing. They're letting me know that they have the right to mess with me, even if they don't have the right to manhandle me the way Ron does.

He takes a large swig of my milkshake. "Well, whatever, that music was pretty BADASS." He eyes Nina. "But we have a strict rule about girlfriends."

Nina eyes him back. "Oh yeah, what's that?"

"No girlfriends."

Nina bursts out laughing. "HA! That's funny!"

Ron giggles, which sounds weird coming out of a very large body. "Nah, I'm just busting your chops. It's all good. As long as your boy toy here remembers that he needs to be all about the TEAM. Job number ONE!" He slaps the top of my head a little too hard. "I know I give this kid a tough time, but that's my job. Especially since the rest of the world seems to think he's some kind of god just because he can throw the football a long way."

I'm not sure what to say, or which direction this conversation is going, so I just keep my mouth shut.

But Nina doesn't.

"I agree, Ron," she says. Then she looks at me and winks. "I don't get why everyone thinks you're such a big deal, Caleb. I mean, it's not like you're saving lives by doing brain surgery, right?"

"Uh, right," I say.

Ron guffaws, which means all of his followers guffaw, too. "I LOVE this girl!" he says, loud enough for everyone in the diner to hear. "I LOVE her!"

And with that, Ron and his crew walk away.

After the dust settles, Nina and I sit quietly for about a minute, absorbing what happened.

"Do you want to get back to what we were talking about?" she says, finally.

"What was that?"

"You were telling me about your dad."

"Oh, that." I check my phone again, in case something fascinating happened in the last thirty seconds. "Uh, nah, I don't think so."

She gives me a long look. "Okay." Then she takes my hand. "If you change your mind, I'm here."

"Thanks."

As we sit there for a little while longer, the quarterback and the singer, I think about her song, and how she was able to nail exactly what we are in just a few words, and how hard that must be.

I couldn't be further from you

You couldn't be further from me

But right next to each other

Is the only place we wanna be

It occurs to me that writing something like that is probably just as hard as throwing a football.

Maybe even harder.

◂11

"I'm sorry."

My dad pauses, then takes a deep breath. It's the next morning, and we're in the basement, lifting weights. I'm on time for my workout, just like I promised I would be.

"About what, Dad?"

"About last night, giving you a hard time about going to that concert. I'm sorry. I should trust you. I *do* trust you."

"It's okay, Dad."

"Was it fun?"

"It was awesome."

"I'm so glad, Cae."

We settle in, and we lift, and it's all good. It's not like lifting weights is a blast, but it's comfortable, it's chill, it's a tradition, it's kind of like breathing.

My mom comes down with a cup of coffee, like always. "So, how was the music?"

"Nina's incredibly talented, Ma. I literally think she might be famous one day."

My dad whistles. "Whoa, that would be some power couple! The Super Bowl quarterback and the rock star."

"Easy there, cowboy," my mom says, and we all laugh.

My dad suddenly stands up. "Well, I gotta go to work," he says.

My mom looks at him. "Work?"

Now it's my dad's turn to look confused. My parents own three car dealerships. My dad is the one who gets all the attention, but my mom is the one who actually runs the business.

"Yeah, hon," he says. "It's Saturday."

"No, honey, it's Sunday." My mom puts her hand on my dad's arm. "The day you work out with Caleb, remember? And then you swim?"

"Oh right!" he says, slapping his hand down on the weight bar. "Of course!"

My mom kisses me on the top of my head and goes back upstairs. My dad and I are left sitting there. It's quiet, but the feeling is different. My dad's mood suddenly seems a little off, maybe because of what just happened.

"I think we're gonna work on some third-down conversion sets this week in practice," I say, bringing the conversation back to football, his comfort zone. "I think we could use a little sharpening up there."

My dad nods. "Good idea. There are still some improvements to be made with the run game, too. You can't be expected to bail out the offense on every drive in every game. The good teams will smell that out a mile away."

"Totally agree."

We keep lifting, and we keep talking about football.

It's where we belong.

And it feels okay.

WALTHORNE NEWS.COM

SATURDAY, OCTOBER 11, 9:14 AM

Freshman Sensation Already Being Recruited? Young QB to Visit State for Game Today

There's been lots of buzz about Caleb Springer, the freshman quarterback who has guided the Walthorne Wildcats to a 4–0 record this year, most recently throwing for two touchdowns and running for one in last night's 41–14 thumping of Praterville. The son of former NFL standout Sammy Springer, young Caleb is already drawing interest from some major college programs. In fact, WalthorneNews has learned that Brandon Williams, an assistant coach and recruiting specialist at State U, has invited Caleb up to campus today to watch the Buzzcocks play Auburn in an exciting matchup. Adding to the speculation is the fact that Williams and the elder Springer were teammates together on the New York Jets for three years, and have remained good friends ever since.

When asked about the rumors at a recent game, Sammy laughed and said, "It's way too early to talk about any college plans for Caleb. He's just concentrating on winning tonight, and then hopefully making it to the playoffs. We're taking it one game at a time, and let's see what happens."

Caleb himself was not made available for comment.

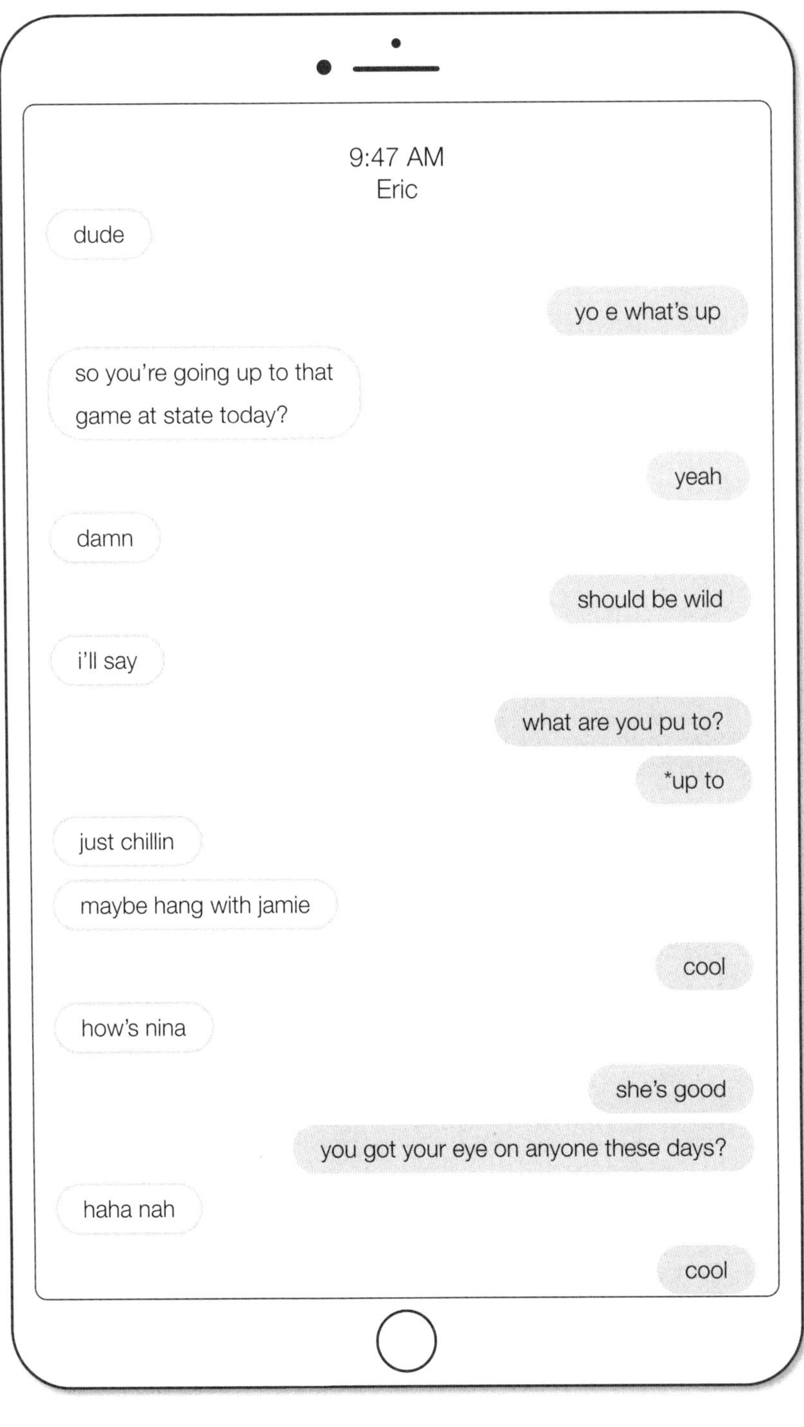
9:47 AM
Eric
dude
yo e what's up
so you're going up to that game at state today?
yeah
damn
should be wild
i'll say
what are you pu to?
*up to
just chillin
maybe hang with jamie
cool
how's nina
she's good
you got your eye on anyone these days?
haha nah
cool

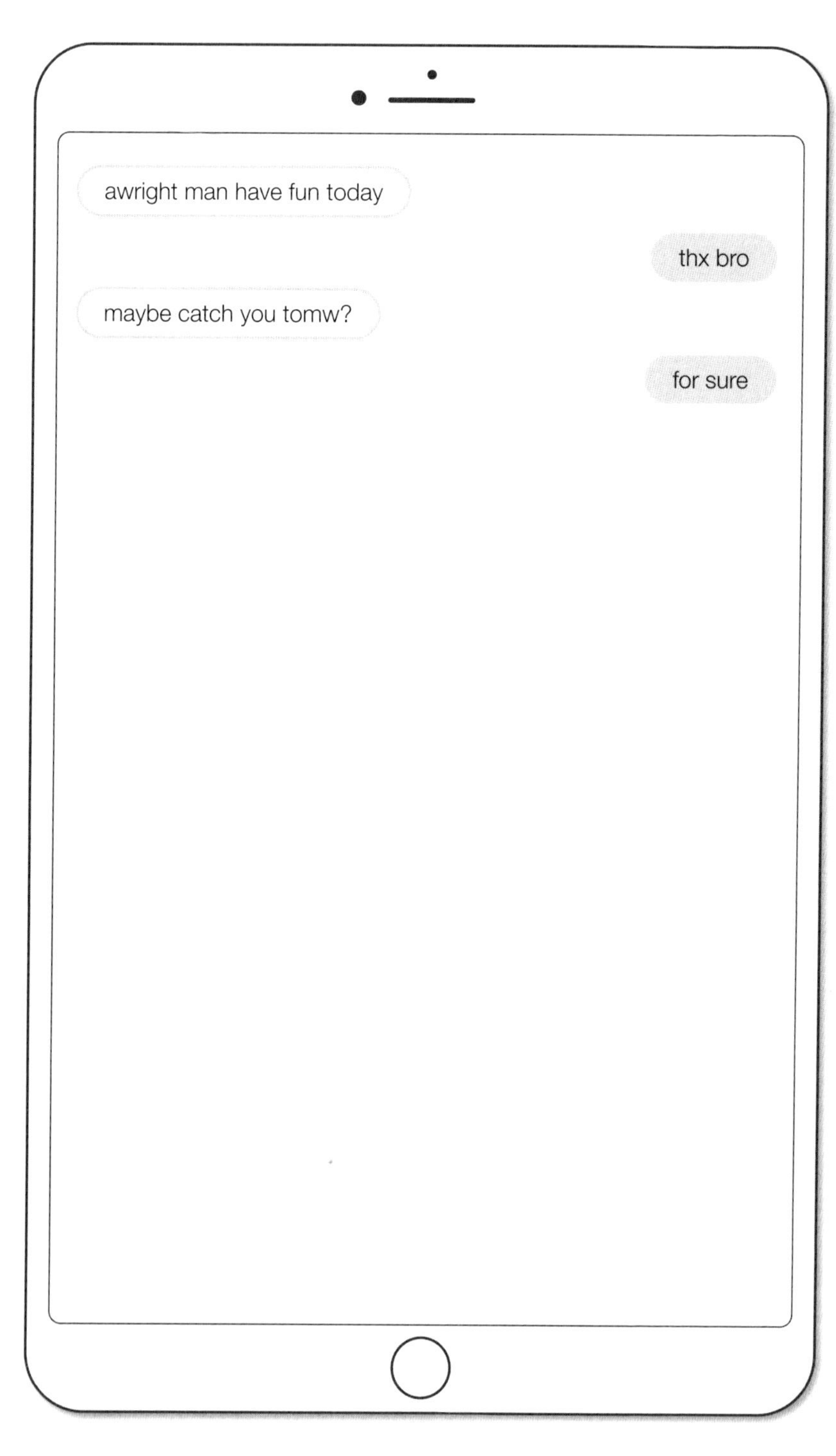
awright man have fun today
thx bro
maybe catch you tomw?
for sure

12

It's a pretty long drive to State. My mom puts on one of those political podcasts she likes to listen to, while my dad closes his eyes. I scroll through my phone, doing some texting, some social media, and trying to find out a little more about Brandon Williams. When I asked my dad about him at breakfast, he just kind of shrugged and said, *Great guy, great football player.* It's funny, my dad doesn't love talking about the old days as much as you might think. The only time he does it is when fans bring it up—which is always. I guess that's why he doesn't like to do it the rest of the time.

"Dad," I say, in the car.

He grunts.

"It says here that Brandon led the league in sacks two years in a row."

"That was when he was with the Rams," my dad mumbles. "I was out of the league by then."

"Oh." Then I ask him, "How come you guys are such good friends? I thought offense guys hang around with other offense guys, and same with the defense."

That gets my dad to open his eyes. "Well, that's true usually, but not always." He turns his head toward the window and squints, as if trying to find a memory that's not quite there. "When he was a rookie, I was in my fifth year. We were on special teams together. Special teams are for veterans who are trying to stick around, and rookies who are trying to make a name for themselves. We're trained to be like heat-seeking missiles, you know, running down the field on punts and kickoffs, just trying to crash into people. Well, there was this one game—against the Falcons, I think it was—we were kicking off to start the second half. I'm next to Brandon, and I'm about to tackle the guy returning the kick when I get blindsided—I mean completely wrecked. Some guy came up and just demolished me; I had no idea he was there. Complete cheap shot, dirty play, he'd be ejected if that happened today. Well, I was barely back on my feet when Brandon popped the guy. Just leveled him. I forget the guy's name, but he'd been in the league for a few years, you know, and was a respected guy, and Brandon was just a kid, but Brandon didn't care, he defended me, and there was this fight, and Brandon got ejected and suspended for two games, meaning he had to give up two weeks of salary, too. The guy did that for me, to protect me."

My dad turns from the window and swivels around to face me, in the back seat. "He's a solid guy. A real solid guy."

I nod, kind of in shock. It's the most my dad has talked to me about his playing days since—well, pretty much since ever. "That's cool," I say. Then, hungry for more, I ask, "I don't think I've ever seen that play on YouTube. Were you, like, injured from the hit? Or were you fine?"

But my dad's eyes are closed again. This time, I think he might be asleep. Or he's pretending to be.

Either way, the conversation is over.

13

It's raining a little, but who cares? The stadium is full and the roar of the crowd is deafening. We're smack on the fifty yard line, in one of those inside-outside boxes where we can watch the game then go inside during breaks to eat from the incredible spread of food that's just sitting there.

And it's all free!

My mom and I watch as my dad says hello to a nonstop stream of people. You can pretty much figure out who the former players are—most of them are huge, and a few of them limp or wear sunglasses. My dad wears sunglasses a lot, too. I used to think it was to avoid being recognized, but my mom says it's because he's really sensitive to light. I guess that happens to a lot of guys who played.

I notice this one guy sitting inside, near the food tables. He's the only person there who's not up and about, mingling and chatting. He must be a pretty big deal because he waits for people to come to him, which is what my dad usually does.

But this time, my dad goes up to him. They talk for around ten minutes, which is a really long time for my dad.

My mom and I are already in our seats by the time my dad comes over to sit down. He points back at the man in the chair. “See that guy? That’s Jimmy Lewis, although everyone calls him Thunder, because that’s what he did. He brought the thunder every time he carried the ball. One of the best tailbacks in history, played right here at State and then had a great career with the Broncos. We overlapped one year in the league.” My dad looks back at him and grins. “Man, it’s so good to see him.”

My mom and I glance at Mr. Lewis, or Thunder, who’s eating a sandwich. It takes him about five seconds to bring the sandwich up to his mouth, and we can tell from here that his hands are pretty shaky. My mom and I glance at each other. I’m pretty sure she’s thinking what I’m thinking. *He doesn’t look so good.*

But we don’t say that to my dad, of course.

The game starts, and on State’s second play from scrimmage, their quarterback, a sophomore named Russell Mangrove, throws a sixty-yard bomb for a touchdown.

I watch Russell as he sprints down the field, joining the celebration in the end zone as the crowd goes nuts. Then he heads back to the sidelines, getting smacks on the helmet from his coaches, before running behind his bench toward the stands and waving his hands upward, as if to say, *More! More! Love me some more!* And the crowd doesn't need to be asked twice. They roar even louder, and keep roaring so loud that the Auburn offense can't hear their quarterback call the signals, which makes them commit a penalty by jumping early, which makes the crowd roar even LOUDER.

I'm watching this whole thing with my parents, and we're going just as bonkers as everyone else, and my dad looks as happy as I've seen him in a long time. I imagine how happy he would be if it were me out there, and I'm sure he's thinking exactly what I'm thinking.

I live for the game.

There's this other thought going through my head, too.

I want this.

I want the glory.

I want the love.

I want it all.

I take a selfie with the field and the rowdy crowd behind me, and I text it to Nina with the caption, Awesome, right?

She texts me back:

are they all cheering for you?

haha very funny

see you tonite?

yup.

I post the pic on Instagram and then keep checking to see how many likes it gets. By the time the game ends, it's at 247. Not bad for a high school freshman.

State wins, 49–20.

14

The first thing that hits you in a college locker room is the smell.

It's a whole different level of stink.

There are wet towels everywhere; random shoes and cleats and pads and mouth guards all over the place; soaked-through, filthy T-shirts lining the floor; and the air is thick with steam and sweat and men's cologne or aftershave or whatever it is.

All things considered, it has to be pretty close to the most disgusting place on earth.

And it's awesome.

My mom wants no part of it, of course; she's waiting outside in the tunnel that leads to the VIP parking lot, where our car is. When my dad and I walk into the locker room, no one pays any attention to us at first, and I realize that a lot of these college players have no idea who my dad is. He played a long time ago, he wasn't that big a star, and he could be just another one of those rich guys who give a lot of money to the program just so he can pretend to know the players.

So we're in the middle of the grossness, trying to avoid discarded jockstraps, when a loud voice behind us booms, "There y'all are! Welcome to the party!"

My dad and I turn around to see Brandon Williams heading for us. He's even bigger than I remembered.

"Great win, Coach," I tell him. "Incredible."

"Lots of things to work on, to be honest," Coach Williams says. "But we'll get there. We got some horses on this team." He throws his arm around my dad's shoulders. "So whaddya say, Dinger? Can you see your boy running around this place someday, making things happen?"

My dad beams. "Oh man, it would be a great fit."

Coach Williams puts one of his giant paws on my shoulder. "Caleb, you want to meet Russell?"

"The QB?"

"That's the one."

"Yeah, sure, that'd be awesome!"

We head over to a corner of the locker room, where Russell Mangrove is talking to a bunch of people with cameras and phones that they're using as tape recorders. They're shouting questions at him, and he's answering each one, quietly, patiently, with a smile, like he's been doing it for a thousand years.

Coach Williams catches his eye, and Russell tells the reporters, "Give me a minute, guys and gals, would you please?" The crowd parts as he slides toward us. He slithers more than walks, kind of like a slow-motion snake. It's like he knows he can take his time, because people will wait for him. It takes him ten seconds to cover the three feet between him and us. Hard to believe that an hour ago he was running all over Auburn, destroying them with his feet and arm.

He looks down at me. "Who's this?"

"Better watch out," Coach Williams says. "This kid's coming for your job."

Russell chuckles. "Nice, a QB! What's your name, bruh?"

"Caleb. Caleb Springer."

"Where you play?"

"Walthorne High."

"Where's that?"

"About four hours from here."

"Sweet." Russell nods. "Well, all I know is Coach Dubs here isn't all that big on bringing high school kids into the locker room, so you must have something nice going on. Keep it up. We'd love to see you here at the Blue House."

"The what?"

Coach Williams laughs. "That's what we call the stadium."

I nod. "You played great," I tell Russell.

"Thanks." He does a few slow stretches, and winces. "Nothing too bad today. Still standing. That's a win in my book, baby. All you can ask for." He glances back at the crowd of people still standing around his locker. "Well, let me go get this over with. These people are like lions in the zoo, man; they won't leave you alone until they've been fed." Russell gives me a fist bump. "Work hard, bruh. Nothing more to say than that. If you got the talent, that's the only thing left. The work."

It takes him another ten seconds to walk the three feet back.

I look at Coach Williams. "Does he walk so slowly because it looks cool, or because it hurts to move?"

"Both," says the coach.

15

"THUNDER! THUNDER!"

I can hear my dad's voice from across the room as Coach Williams introduces me to some other players, a few coaches, and one of the team's student managers, a girl named Stacey. "She's forgotten more about football than you'll ever know," Coach tells me when he introduces us.

Everyone is incredibly friendly. They're all in a great mood because the team won big, of course, but I can tell they're also being super nice because when Coach Williams brings someone around, it's for one reason and one reason only. To make that someone fall in love with State football.

It's totally working on me.

I'm just finishing talking to the quarterbacks' coach when my dad's voice booms again. "THUNDER! Come meet my kid!"

They're heading toward me. I notice all the players stop what they're doing and watch. They didn't know who my dad was, but they definitely know who Jimmy "Thunder" Lewis is.

Thunder seems to be walking okay, but his hands are shaking.

"This the kid?" Thunder says when he reaches me. "Gotta be. He looks like you."

My dad looks as proud as I've ever seen him. "Caleb, I want you to meet one of the greatest football players ever, one of the toughest football players ever, and a Hall of Famer, James 'Thunder' Lewis. Jimmy, this is my son, Caleb."

Jimmy raises his hand, and I shake it. He's a big man, but his grip is weak.

"What did you say your name was again, son?"

"Caleb."

"Ah right. You a running back?"

"Quarterback."

"Good for you." He looks over at my dad. "Just like his old man, that right?"

My dad clears his throat. "Uh, actually, Thunder, I played wideout for the Jets, remember? We had that one season together in the league. Greatest honor of my life, being on the same field as you."

Thunder scratches his head. "Oh yeah, brother, sure, sure. What did you say your name was again?"

No one seems to know who he's asking, so I decide it's me.

"Oh, uh, sorry. It's Caleb."

"Caleb, right." He squints over at my dad. "This your pop? What's his name, then?"

My dad shifts uncomfortably on his feet. "Thunder, buddy, it's me, Sammy. Dinger. We've been—you know, we've been talking about the old times. It's so good to see you, man."

Thunder's eyes flicker with recognition. "Oh yeah, brother, so good to see you, too." He laughs—a tired laugh—and winks at me. "These days, I call most men 'brother' and most women 'sister.' Just easier, you know what I mean?"

"I sure do, Mr. Lewis."

He pretends to be mad. "Hey now, you call me Thunder!"

For the first time, I notice a young woman standing a few feet away, and I realize she's watching Thunder closely. She slides past a few people until she's next to him. "Dad, you getting tired?" she asks him, softly. "We should go. It's been a long day."

"Oh yeah, honey," Thunder says. "It has. It's been a long day. It's been a real long day. But a good day, right?"

"A great day."

"We going to the game, then?"

Thunder's daughter seems completely unfazed by this question. "The game just ended, Daddy. State won big."

His face lights up. "Oh, that's great! That's just great, baby."

She gently takes his arm and starts guiding him out of the room. Brandon runs interference for them, protecting their path like an offensive lineman.

"We're honored you came out today, Thunder," Brandon says. "The boys on the team are never gonna forget it."

"See you soon, brother," Thunder says to no one and everyone. Then he slowly walks away, with his daughter holding his arm.

I'm standing next to my dad, waiting for him to tell us what to do or where to go. I figure we're going to follow them out. But instead, he just stands there, watching them.

"Dad?" I ask him, after a minute. "Should, uh, should we go, too?"

"Yeah," he says, still looking straight ahead. "Let's go find Mom."

We say goodbye to a few people and leave the locker room. Outside, we look for Coach Williams, but he's not around.

My mom is waiting by the exit, and when she sees us, she comes running over. "How was it?" she asks, excitedly. "Was it awesome? Did you meet some of the players?"

"It was cool," I say. "I met the quarterback. He seems really nice. He told me to keep working hard." I'm trying to sound enthusiastic, but my mom can tell there's something off about my voice.

She turns to my dad. "Everything okay?"

But he doesn't answer. He just gives her one of his grunts that means, *I don't want to talk about it.*

My mom gets the message.

We head out to the VIP parking lot. It's not very big, but we still can't find the car.

"You were supposed to take a picture of where we parked," my dad says to my mom. "Damn it, honey, I told you that like five times."

"I forgot," she says.

"I hate it when you forget things," my dad says.

My mom finds the car two minutes later. My dad looks at her with nothing but love in his eyes.

"I don't know what I'd do without you," he says.

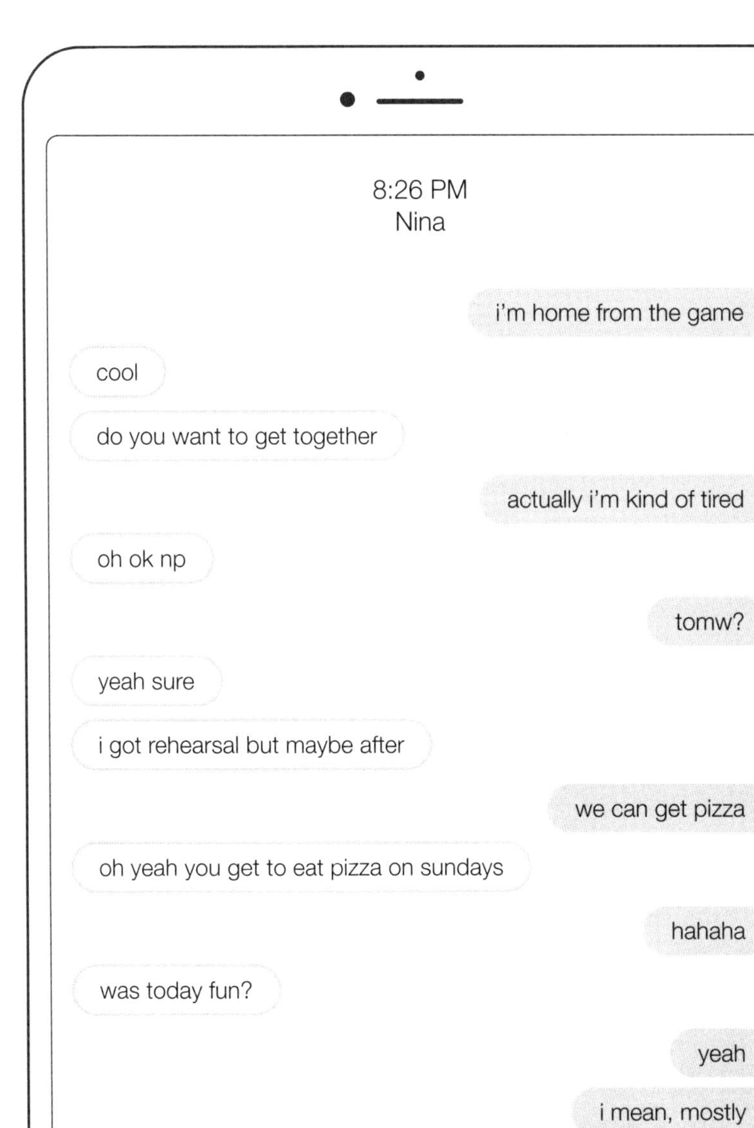
8:26 PM
Nina
i'm home from the game
cool
do you want to get together
actually i'm kind of tired
oh ok np
tomw?
yeah sure
i got rehearsal but maybe after
we can get pizza
oh yeah you get to eat pizza on sundays
hahaha
was today fun?
yeah
i mean, mostly
also a little weird
what do you mean

nothing really
see you tomorrew
*tomorrow
ok sleep well

16

After dinner, in my room, I flip open my laptop.

I go to YouTube.

First, I type in "Jimmy Thunder Lewis highlights."

I watch about ten minutes of Thunder carrying or catching the ball, bulling his way for extra yards, dragging defenders, faking them out of their shoes, and getting hit. Hit high, hit low, hit late, hit often, hit in the head.

Some of it hurts just watching it.

I close the laptop.

I lie back on my bed. I need to do some homework, but I'm not sure I can concentrate.

Finally, I go back to the laptop, back to YouTube.

This time I type in, "Sammy Springer hardest hits."

A bunch of videos pop up immediately, including some I recognize. I start scrolling through them—a greatest hits of hits. I watch my dad getting popped, bumped, dumped, smacked, crushed, smushed, totaled. The touchdown catch against the

Browns in '02 is one of the biggest shots he takes. But then I find a video I've never seen before.

It's called "HUMAN WEEBLE: DINGER SPRINGER."

I have no idea what a "weeble" is, but of course I click on the link.

⁘⁘⁘

YOUTUBE VIDEO

Human Weeble: After Getting Leveled by Tremaine, Springer Wobbles But Doesn't Fall Down, 12.7.2005

ANNCR 1: . . . the way the Jets are playing, you wouldn't know they're already pretty much out of playoff contention.

ANNCR 2: Say what you will about this team, Jeff. They come to play every week. They compete, they fight hard, and if they're going to go down, they want to go down swinging.

ANNCR 1: The Jets break the huddle with a two-wide set. Heath is split out to the left, Springer to the right. Derek

Adams is the lone setback. Ball is snapped . . . Evans looks to Springer over the middle . . . Pass is a little high . . . Springer reaches up and . . . oh my!

ANNCR 2: WHOA!

ANNCR 1: Tremaine came flying in from the strong safety position and just destroyed Sammy Springer . . .

ANNCR 2: He never saw that coming, Jeff. He was a dead duck right there.

ANNCR 1: Looks like shoulder-to-head contact, Andy. That's a clean hit, but holy smokes, that cannot feel good.

ANNCR 2: Springer looks a little wobbly, Jeff.

ANNCR 1: He sure does, and can you blame him?

ANNCR 2: No, I cannot.

ANNCR 1: Sammy Springer getting a little help as he heads to the sidelines. He's going to have to sit out a play or two here, I would think.

⁂

I stare at the video of my dad weaving unsteadily to the sidelines, with one thought going through my aching head:

I recognize that walk.

It's the same walk Thunder Lewis had in a few of the clips I just watched.

⁂

ANNCR 2:	Maybe so, but if I know Dinger Springer, he's going to want to get right back out there. That's just how he's wired.
ANNCR 1:	He's taken some real hard shots over the years, but he always seems to bounce right back. He is some kind of warrior, there's no doubt about that. Listen to the hand he's getting as he makes his way to the bench.
ANNCR 2:	Sammy Springer is a credit to the game of football.

⁂

I shut my laptop while the video is still playing, because I know how the story ends.

My dad retired two weeks later.

I text Nina:

i think maybe you were right

Then I turn my phone off before I have a chance to read her reply.

17

"So, what was that about, last night?"

We're sitting at Slice of Life, my favorite pizza place, and Nina is doing something she's really good at: not letting me off the hook.

"What was what about?"

She rolls her eyes, because she knows I know exactly what she's referring to.

"Texting me, then ghosting me."

"I didn't ghost you! I fell asleep."

"I texted you back in two seconds. You fell asleep in two seconds?"

"I was tired."

"Right. Sure."

I finish one slice and dig into another.

"So," she says again, "I was right about what?"

"Do we have to talk about this now?"

"CALEB!" she says, in her no-nonsense voice. "You keep bringing it up, then saying you don't want to talk about it, then texting me, then ignoring me. Enough! Spit it out!"

"Okay, fine." I eat as slowly as I possibly can, while she waits patiently. "My dad . . . It's like his brain goes on vacation sometimes. Like, one minute he's totally there, and he's my dad, and he's great, and the next minute he's screaming for no reason, or he's threatening to beat up some drunk fan, or he can't remember something he said, like, five seconds earlier. It's scary. I can tell my mom is scared, too. But then it's over and he's fine, like, back to normal. I don't— I'm not sure what to do."

Nina's eyes change as I'm talking. They start out gentle, understanding; then they turn colder, and I see anger.

"You know what this is, right?"

"What do you mean?"

"It's obvious. It's football. This is your dad having, like, some delayed reaction from getting the crap beat out of him for years."

"We don't know that for sure."

"You wrote that you agreed with me!"

"I wrote maybe!"

We both take a deep breath.

"What else could it be?" Nina asks, in a softer voice.

"I know a ton of retired football players who are doing great," I say, which isn't exactly an answer to her question. "My dad's friends. Brandon, the guy who coaches up at State." I don't mention Jimmy "Thunder" Lewis. I don't have the guts to say it out loud—to her, or to myself.

"Okay, sure, fine," she says.

I take a sip of root beer. "It could be like I said, just extra stress, related to the season and all the pressure I'm under."

"Whatever you want to tell yourself, Caleb. I know you love the game more than anything, but you need to think about this. For real."

"Think about what?"

She hesitates for a split second before speaking. "About playing. About sticking with football."

Even though I knew that's what she was going to say, I'm still shocked. "Are you serious right now? I knew I shouldn't have said anything to you about this!" Nina's eyes look wounded, and I realize I'm getting way too wound up, so I try to calm down. "Listen, Nina, that was a totally different time. The game is so safe now. They come out with new equipment every year designed especially to protect the players!"

She doesn't answer right away, and I don't say anything, and it's quiet. I mean, not quiet, exactly, because we're in a crowded pizza place. Then suddenly she gets up and starts to walk away. I'm deciding whether to go after her when she turns around and comes back to the table. But she doesn't sit down. Instead, she stands over me.

"So that's it then, Caleb? You're going to just keep playing and allow your body and brain to get destroyed?"

I look up at her. "How did this become about me?"

"Because I don't want you to end up like your dad, that's how."

I stand up, too, so we're face-to-face. "My dad is awesome! He's a freakin' legend and a superstar! I would be, like, completely honored to end up like my dad!"

I stop talking. Actually, I stop yelling. I notice I'm breathing hard. I sit back down. Nina sits back down. We watch each other. She suddenly takes my face in her hands, and I lean into them. It's the most intimate physical thing we've ever done.

"I didn't mean anything bad about your dad, Caleb. I'm sorry if it came off that way. I just meant—you could stop playing football if you wanted to. You could save yourself from the danger of the same thing happening to you."

I close my eyes for a few seconds, because if I leave them open, I think there might be some tears to deal with. "Stop playing football?" I can't even believe I'm saying those words out loud. Life without football doesn't seem possible. "I'm the starting varsity quarterback and we're in the middle of the season, in case you haven't noticed."

Nina leans in close and speaks softly. "I know how important football is to you. I know how much you love it, and I know how good you are at it."

"So then why are you trying to take it away from me?" The words are out of my mouth before I can stop them.

Nina's eyes harden again, and I suddenly get the panicky feeling that I blew it for real this time. "I'm not trying to take anything from you," she says, staring me square in the eyes. "But I know what might happen if you keep playing. And so do you."

I'm having one of those moments when there is so much going on in my mind that nothing is going on in my mind.

"I don't want to talk about this anymore," I tell her. "I'm sorry I brought it up."

Nina's eyes lock onto mine.

"Are you?" she asks.

This time, she really does leave.

WALTHORNENEWS.COM

WELCOME TO THE JUNGLE
A HIGH SCHOOL SPORTS BLOG ABOUT
THE WALTHORNE WILDCATS
BY ALFIE JENKS
SUNDAY, OCTOBER 26

Football Team Continues to Dominate; Frosh QB Leads the Way

A few months ago, at the beginning of the football season, Walthorne High School's varsity football coach William Toffler wasn't about to put too much pressure on his freshman quarterback, Caleb Springer. "He's young, so let's not get ahead of ourselves," he told me at the time. "This is high school football, and even the most talented kids need a little time to get used to it."

Well, here we are just past the halfway mark for the season, and it's become clearer with each passing game (pun intended) that Caleb Springer isn't your average "talented kid." Sporting a 6–0 record, the Wildcats have the whole town buzzing. They've been led by an offense that's averaging 38 points a game, behind Springer's passing and running talents. "It seems like every week, he does something that just basically shocks us," says Coach Toffler. "I've been coaching a long time, and even I can't believe some of the throws he makes, or how he scrambles out of trouble. I gotta believe this kid is pretty much the best QB in the history of Walthorne."

That may be getting ahead of ourselves, but right now, Caleb is averaging 269 passing yards and 53 rushing yards a game, both of which would put him in the history books as top five all-time at Walthorne High. And the fact that he's a freshman makes it even more amazing.

"I mean, he comes from a football family, and his dad was a total superstar, so I guess I shouldn't be too surprised," added the coach. "This kid is in a league of his own, and he's only going to get better. All I can say is, I feel bad for the other teams in this league for the next four years." Then he laughed and said, "Well, actually not that bad.

I asked Caleb for a comment, and as usual, he was humble. "I'm just really lucky to be part of such a good team, with great coaching, and an unbelievable offensive line," he said. "Ron and the guys give me all day to throw the ball. Without them I'd be lost out there. Oh man, I'm late for bio, gotta go." Then he walked away, already a star, but just a regular kid, too.

18

I'm at the store, buying some compression shorts.

While I wait in line, I notice this guy staring at me like he knows me. He looks like he's around my dad's age, and I have no idea who he is. A few weeks ago, I might have been creeped out by the guy, but at this point I know what's coming.

Sure enough, a few seconds later he breaks out in this big grin. "I knew it was you! Caleb Springer, right?"

"Nailed it," I say, which is something I've heard my dad say to people when they recognize him.

The guy looks like he hit the lottery. "Man, it's so cool to meet you. I saw the game last week against Branchville—you were on fire! That third-quarter touchdown pass was a total DIME!"

"Thanks, man, thanks a lot. We did some good things in that game."

The guy grabs his phone. "You cool with a selfie? My kids are gonna love this!"

"Yeah, no problem," I say. I'm thinking how weird it is that this guy is acting like I'm the best thing that ever happened to him, and I'm also thinking how it's even weirder that I'm getting so used to it.

He snaps the picture, then starts pumping my hand. "Great to meet you. Good luck this weekend!"

"Yeah, thanks."

The guy leaves, I go to pay for my shorts, and the woman who works there gives me a smile. "It's wild, right?" she says. "People around here treat high school football players like rock stars."

"We *are* rock stars," I say to her, and we both laugh, because she knows I'm kidding, even though I'm kind of not.

Biking home, I think about what the salesperson said. It's true, the crowds have gotten bigger at every game. They were big at the beginning of the season, but now they're overflowing, with every seat filled and people standing around the edges of the field. You see signs up around town—at the community center, in store windows, tacked up on telephone poles—all cheering on the Walthorne Wildcats.

It's like our team's success is the town's success, and so everyone kind of lives through you and looks up to you and loves you.

I'm not gonna lie, it's fun.

One time I asked Coach Toffler why football was such a huge deal in Walthorne, and he said, "Well, that's how it goes around here. Life is hard, so people need something to feel good about. It just so happens that high school football is easy to feel good about when you win every game."

"But what happens if we lose?" I asked.

Coach laughed. "Then you better run for your life. I'll be right behind you."

School is different, too. The other kids are different. A few days after my argument with Nina, I'm sitting at lunch with Eric and Jamie. The next thing you know, these two girls come up to us. I don't know who they are, and I've never seen them before. The only thing I know for sure is that they're older than us. Maybe even two or three grades older.

"Hey," the shorter, blond one says.

"Hey," the taller, brown-haired one says.

"Hey," we all say.

Okay, so we got the heys out of the way.

The taller girl says, "Which one of you is Caleb?"

Jamie and Eric give each other a look, like, *Here we go again.* "He is," says Jamie, pointing at me.

The shorter girl sits down next to me. "I'm Shawna. It's really nice to meet you. I'm a huge fan."

Eric says, "Uh, how can you be a huge fan if you didn't even know what he looked like?"

Shawna giggles. "Well, usually he has a helmet on, doesn't he?"

"I'm also a football player," Jamie says.

"And I play basketball," Eric adds.

"Super," says Shawna, dismissively. The two girls are focused on me. I don't want to sound cocky, but that's just a fact.

The taller girl starts looking at Jamie, who stares back at her hopefully. But then he figures out that she just wants to sit in his chair, so he gets up. Poor guy.

"I'm Camille," she tells me. "Ron told us that you're, like, going to the pros in football."

I try to laugh, but no sound comes out. "I, uh, well, I don't know about that. Uh, I'm just trying to help us get to the playoffs."

That makes the two girls crack up, as if I just said the funniest thing in the world.

"You are SO CUTE!" says Shawna.

Camille takes one of my french fries. "Mmmm, delicious," she says, even though they're soggy and not delicious at all.

Both girls get up as suddenly as they sat down. "We gotta go," Shawna says.

Camille stretches like a cat after a nap. "So, Caleb," she purrs, "sometimes we get together at my house after the Friday night games. Just a few close friends. Could you come, or is that past your bedtime?"

"I don't have a bedtime," I say, like a dummy.

The girls find that hilarious, too, of course. "Ooh, big boy, all grown up," Camille titters. She sticks her hand out. "Hand me your phone." I do. She types, then hands it back. "I just texted myself from your phone. I'll text you when we have the next party. Hope to see you."

Shawna glances at Eric and Jamie. "And you can bring your backup dancers, if you want," she says.

The girls walk away. The guys stare at them, then at me.

"Hanging around with you is getting more brutal every day," Eric says.

"What the hell was that about?" Jamie adds.

I feel bad for them, but not so bad that it ruins my mood.

"I have no idea," I say, "but you guys better start practicing your dance moves."

1:02 PM
Nina

i saw that

you saw what

those two girls

oh that hahaha

what did they want

nothing.

they were just goofing around

huh

they invited me to some party they might have but i'm not going of course

why not?

you should totally go

during the season?

no way

my dad would disown me

oh so that's why you're not going?

hahaha

okay
mr. heartthrob
cut it out

19

At night is when the doubt creeps in.

After the school day, when everyone treats me like a celebrity, and after practice, when I run the offense on the top-ranked high school team in the state and the seventh-ranked high school team in the country, and after getting home, where I check out social media, do a little homework but mostly just hang out, after all that is over, then it's nighttime, and my parents come home from work, and everything changes.

Tonight, it changes when we sit down for dinner and my dad asks my mom to pass the bacon.

"There is no bacon, honey," she tells him.

"Why not?"

"Well, because it's dinnertime. We just came home from work, remember? But I can make you some if you want." I notice that my mom's tone of voice is like a mother talking to her seven-year-old.

My dad looks irritated. “I don’t want any bacon. Of course it’s dinnertime. I knew that.” I can’t tell if he’s mad at himself, or my mom. Probably both.

“I made mashed potatoes, though,” my mom says. “Your favorite.”

My dad looks genuinely touched. “Thank you, honey. I love mashed potatoes.” He gives my mom’s hand a squeeze, then he looks at me. “Caleb, I have some exciting news. I want you to make a commercial with me.”

I stop chewing. “A what?”

“A commercial, for the dealership. We’re shooting one next week and I want you to be in it. I want to show off the new star quarterback of the next state championship team and future college national champion and NFL Hall of Famer. You’re the new town hero, so it’ll be good for business.”

“Uh, okay, Dad, but, uh, I’ve never been in a commercial before.”

“It’s easy,” my dad says. “Just look into the camera and say the lines. You’re a good-looking kid. You’re a stud. Everyone knows it, right? I mean, why else would that singer girl want to get with you, right? Have you gotten with her yet?”

"Sam, that's ENOUGH." My mother has been really patient with my dad over the last few months, but even she has her limits.

My dad suddenly deflates like a balloon. He sits back in his chair, spent. "Let's have some dessert and then go watch a little TV," he says, softly. "It's been a long day."

It's only when my heart rate slows down that I realize how fast it was beating.

10:23 PM
3 People

you guys good?

JAMIE

whaddya mean?

ERIC

yeah what's up

i acted like an ass at lunch sorry bout that

JAMIE

you mean with those girls? nah man it's all good, it was funny

it was just a goof

JAMIE

i'd like some of that goof just once

ERIC

same

you're just lucky nina wasn't there

yeah you aint lyin, she saw tho
and i mean she's already mad at me as it is

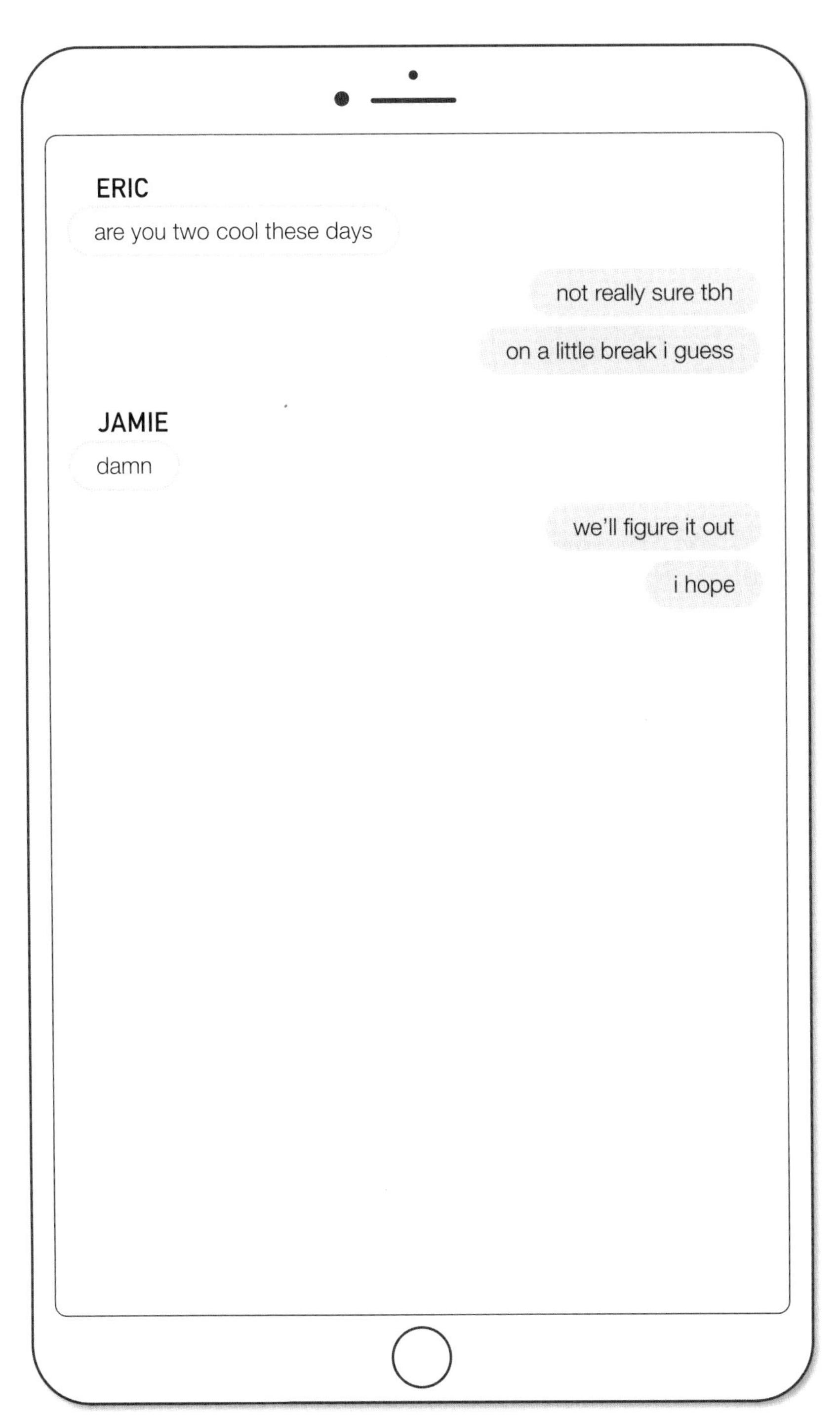
ERIC
are you two cool these days
not really sure tbh
on a little break i guess
JAMIE
damn
we'll figure it out
i hope

Walthorne High vs. Ramsdale High
Season Record: 8–0

WWHS
WALTHORNE HIGH SCHOOL RADIO
TRANSCRIPT OF PLAY-BY-PLAY
ALFIE JENKS AND JULIAN HESS

ALFIE: Hello and welcome everyone to the final regular season game, with the 8–0 Walthorne Wildcats going up today against the 5–3 Ramsdale Rams. At stake today is not only an undefeated record for the Wildcats, but the number one seed in the playoffs . . . Walthorne has gotten off to a fast start this afternoon, with freshman phenom Caleb Springer completing his first seven passes, including a fourteen-yard touchdown strike to one of his favorite targets, tight end Amir Watkins . . .

JULIAN: I saw Amir in the hallway the other day. He is one big dude.

ALFIE: Yes, he is, Julian. Anyway, Caleb looks more and more comfortable back there every game, and the idea that he has three more high school seasons ahead of him must make every coach in this conference quake with fear . . .

JULIAN: I don't agree, Alfie.

ALFIE: Wait, really? Why not?

JULIAN: It makes every coach in the STATE quake with fear!

ALFIE: Oh right.

JULIAN: Nailed it!

ALFIE: Julian, can you try to take this a little more seriously?

JULIAN: Hold up, Alfie. Aren't you the one who's famous for saying sports should be fun? So let's have some fun!

ALFIE: Uh—

JULIAN: Wait, is the great Alfie Jenks speechless?

ALFIE: Of course not.

JULIAN: Could have fooled me.

ALFIE: You're being annoying.

JULIAN: Thank you.

⁘ ⁘ ⁘

The offense is firing on all cylinders in this game, and we're up at the half, 27–6. Coach spends most of his halftime talk focusing on the defense, and the fact that Ramsdale's tailback has broken off a couple of long runs. I sit at my locker, alone. We're not supposed to use our phones at all during games, but I decide to try to sneak in a quick text to Nina.

i'm pretty sure I know the answer to this, but are you at the game today?

Two seconds later, I add:

i miss u

I'm waiting for her to answer when Ron comes up to me. "Wait, were you just using your PHONE?"

"Uh—"

"Are you serious right now? You think the rules don't apply to you? Come on, dude, that's BULL!"

"I'm really sorry."

Ron grabs the phone. "Who were you texting?"

"No one. Just a friend."

"Was it that singer chick?"

"None of your business."

"Are you sure? What's your password, dude?"

"Ron, cut it out." I try to grab the phone back, but he holds it out of reach. "Give it back!" I say louder.

A couple of the other guys start to gather around, laughing at the sight of me trying to grab my phone like a little kid.

"Aw, give him his toy," says Jason Kimball, another offensive lineman. "He wants to go out and play." But instead, Ron throws the phone to Jason, who throws it to this other kid, Chet, who throws it back to Ron.

This goes on for a few more minutes until Coach Toffler wanders over to find out what all the commotion is about. "What the HELL, boys?!" he hollers. "You're supposed to be saving your energy for the second half!" Coach spots the phone in Ron's hand. "Are you kidding me right now? Are you a bunch of three-year-olds? You know there's no phones during games!"

Ron wouldn't rat me out, but I decide to step up. "Sorry,

Coach, it's my phone," I say. "Ron was just reminding me about the no-phone rule. I'm real sorry."

Coach Toffler walks up to Ron and snatches the phone out of his hands. I fully expect him to ream me out, but instead, he lays into Ron. "So you decide to teach him a lesson by playing keep-away with his phone? How old are you, anyway? Show some leadership, Johnson!" Coach throws me the phone, but I drop it. "Damn good thing you're not a receiver, son," he says, then winks at me before walking back to the coaches' office.

Everyone drifts away, except for Ron, who's standing there red-faced. "Well, well. Boy Wonder has truly arrived. You're untouchable now. Even the coaches won't mess with you." Then he leans into me, eyes flaring. "If you're not careful, someone is going to kick the snot out of that cocky little head of yours. In the meantime, just keep winning and we're all good."

I look down at my phone and spot a crack in the glass. I curse silently, knowing my parents are going to make me pay for it. I stare at the broken screen, and right then a text comes in from Nina.

are you allowed to send texts during a game?

WWHS
WALTHORNE HIGH SCHOOL RADIO
TRANSCRIPT OF PLAY-BY-PLAY
ALFIE JENKS AND JULIAN HESS

ALFIE: We're midway through the third quarter, and Walthorne has been dominating play. With the score 43–13, we can look for Coach Toffler to start putting in some of the backups, but for now, Caleb Springer continues to lead the offense, and they're on the march once again . . . It's a first and ten on the Ramsdale thirty-two, and he swings a screen pass out to Ethan Metzger . . . Freshman Kenny Coleman is out front, leading the way . . . Metzger breaks one tackle and heads for the first-down marker . . . Oh, Coleman gets hit HARD as he tries to make a block!

JULIAN: Kenny Coleman is down, Alfie . . . Now he's on his feet, but we'll have to keep an eye on him . . .

⁜⁜⁜

I can hear the *CRACK!* when Kenny gets hit, and I know it's pretty bad right away. The rules are clear—helmet-to-helmet contact is not allowed—but sometimes when two guys are going in opposite directions at full speed, the helmets just get in the way.

No one is trying to hurt anyone, but people get hurt anyway.

That's football.

After the hit, Kenny gets up and acts like everything is fine. It's what football players do.

Kenny runs back to the huddle, and Ron smacks him on the shoulder pads, just like he did with me when I took that hard hit in the first game of the season. "You good?"

Kenny nods. "Yeah, yeah, all good."

"Excellent!" Ron says. "Way to be tough!"

"You sure?" I say to Kenny, but he doesn't answer. As I'm trying to figure out what to do, Brett Rose brings in the play from the sidelines. "Twenty-Four Scramble Brick Left." Which is a complicated way of saying a run to the left side. Kenny's side. Which means he's going to get leveled again.

As we break the huddle, I notice Kenny still standing there. "What's up?" I ask him.

It's hard to see his eyes through his helmet, but his voice sounds off. "What's the play again?"

I start to tell him. "Twenty-Four Scramble—" Then I stop, and tell him, "QB Keep, QB Keep."

He nods, and takes his position. The team lines up. "PINEAPPLE!" I scream out, meaning I'm changing the play at the line of scrimmage. "STRAIGHT CHASE FOURTEEN! STRAIGHT CHASE FOURTEEN!" Which means a quarterback sneak, or keep.

Ron looks back at me. "What the hell?"

"That's the play," I tell him. "HUT!"

He snaps the ball, but it's clear that some of our linemen didn't hear me. They all start drifting left, ready to block, which leaves just me and Ron staring at their entire defense. I try to run behind Ron's right shoulder, but only gain about half a yard before getting smothered by their middle linebacker and two other guys. Luckily, they're clean hits, and I'm totally fine.

I pop back up just in time to see Coach Toffler sprinting out onto the field, way beyond where he's supposed to go. "SPRINGER! WHAT THE HELL ARE YOU DOING RUNNING A SNEAK! YOU COULD HAVE GOTTEN KILLED!"

I ignore his question and point at Kenny instead. "He's gotta come out."

Coach looks confused. "Who, Kenny? Why?"

"Because he's not right. He's hurt. He took a real shot on the last play."

Coach calls a time-out, and everyone runs over to the sideline to grab water. Coach goes up to Kenny. "What's going on? Are you hurt? You get hurt on that hit?"

"Nah, I'm good!" Kenny insists. Then, as if to prove it, he adds, "I'll get a break at halftime, Coach. It's fine!"

Coach glances quickly over at our trainer, then puts his arm around Kenny. "Well, we've already had halftime, son. So let's go over and take a little break now—what do you say?"

Kenny nods, like a little kid. "Sure thing, Coach. Sure thing."

The rest of the guys have their heads down. No one wants to watch, but everyone wants to listen.

The ref blows the whistle, and we head back out onto the field. We huddle up, and Ron does what he always does when we come back from a time-out, which is to clap his hands and start yelling. "Let's get after it, boys! Let's get AFTER IT!"

But this time, I interrupt him. "Ron, are you serious right now? 'Let's get after it'?"

He glares at me. "You got a problem, Springer?

You're sitting there, a freakin' freshman acting like the coach and the captain all rolled into one, and you're asking ME if I'M SERIOUS?"

"Yeah, I got a problem," I say. The rest of the team falls dead silent. No one talks to Ron this way—especially a freshman—but something inside of me doesn't care about that right now.

"If you don't want me to act like the captain," I tell him, "then *you* be the captain! You need to look out for the players. Kenny got rocked, he was clearly messed up, and you didn't care. You asked him if he was okay—what do you think he's gonna say? Of course he's going to say he's okay! And then you let him line up for the next play? That's bullshit, and you know it. He could've gotten seriously hurt. He might be seriously hurt right now. And you were fine with it! Because that's football, right?"

Ron is something I've never seen him be before—speechless. It's like he's so mad, he forgot how to talk. His eyes are burning into mine, but he doesn't say a word.

One of the other seniors, an overweight but quick lineman named Seamus, says, "Caleb, you need to shut up. Everyone needs to shut up. We got a game to play." Of course he throws a few swear words in along the way. More than a few, actually.

The ref blows his whistle. "DELAY OF GAME!" We get penalized five yards.

Coach Toffler starts jumping up and down. He's literally hopping mad. "RUN THE PLAY!" he keeps screaming. "RUN THE DAMN PLAY!"

Eventually, we do. It's a sweep wide right. We score, and there are a few high fives, but something's missing. Something's changed.

When I run to the sideline, Coach doesn't even look at me. He just says, very softly, "Take a seat. You're done for the day."

Fine by me.

We win, 49–20. In the locker room, no one celebrates.

20

"Why'd you come out?"

My dad has me cornered in that section of the parking lot he hangs out in, and he's peppering me with questions.

"What did Coach say to you during that time-out? What was going on there? He seemed upset—why was he upset?"

I'm used to his questions after the game, and usually I answer them all. But today, I'm not really in the mood. "Dad, we won big. We were running up the score. Kenny got hurt on a pass play. Why are we even passing at all when we're up thirty? I was glad to come out."

My dad shakes his head in disgust. "No one should ever be glad to come out."

"I thought you played great," says my mom. I see her looking around, wondering who might be eavesdropping. She's always been a private person, which isn't easy when your husband is a local celebrity.

"He played good for two and a half quarters," my dad says. "After that, no sign of him! Maybe I should talk to the coach."

"Don't do that!" I say quickly. "Please. Let me handle it."

"Handle what?" I hear a voice say behind me.

A female voice.

A voice I know.

I turn around to see Nina, with a not-quite-smile on her face. "Hey," she says. "Handle what?"

I'm shocked to see her, and I find myself moving to put myself between her and my dad. "Wait a second, were you at the game?"

"Saw some of the second half. So exciting. Not." She leans in to speak softly. "Did you actually text me at halftime? Isn't that illegal or something? Is that why you weren't playing?"

"Kind of but not really," I tell her. "The whole game was weird. I sort of got in trouble."

My dad hears that. "Trouble? What kind of trouble?"

"Nothing, Dad."

He notices Nina. "Who are you?"

Before she can answer, I do. "This is Nina, Dad."

"Who?"

"Nina Rojas. My friend, remember? I told you about her."

My dad frowns. "No, I don't remember."

"She's a musician, Dad. I went to see her play."

"Oh yeah," he says.

My mom steps up. "So nice to meet you, Nina! Caleb speaks so highly of you. You must be a very special girl."

Nina smiles shyly. "Oh, I don't know about that."

"What did you think?" my dad asks Nina. "Did you think Caleb should have been taken out of the game in the third quarter?"

"Uh, I . . ." Nina looks at me for help.

"She came late, Dad," I say.

But he's not going to let it go. "She was there; she can answer for herself." He looks over at Nina. "Well?"

Nina straightens her back, and I suddenly know what's coming. You only get shy, quiet Nina for so long.

"Well, to be honest, Mr. Springer, I'm not a huge fan of football."

My dad looks confused. "Excuse me?"

"I don't get it at all. The rules are really confusing. And I think it's dangerous."

I feel my body tense up, waiting for Nina to say more, to go into all the stuff that we talked about, the stuff about how what's happening to my dad could end up happening to me, the stuff that made us get into our first real fight.

But she doesn't. She doesn't say anything else.

My dad isn't sure what to make of this girl, and my mom grabs his arm to make sure he stays in control. Eventually, he just shakes his head and starts to walk away, but then he turns back.

"Life is dangerous," he says, loud enough for anyone around to hear. "Get used to it."

My mom and dad head off in the direction of some other parents, who are talking about the game. I look at Nina. "I hope he's not going to talk to the coach," I tell her. "That would not be good."

"I don't want to talk about football anymore," Nina says.

"Yeah, me neither." A few seconds later, I add, "So, uh, why did you come?"

"You asked me to."

"You mean that text? I just asked if you were here."

"Well, I took it to mean, 'I hope you're here.' So I came."

"Oh."

I watch as my parents talk to some other people. Nina watches me watch them.

I turn back to her. "Hey, how's the band going?"

"It's going great," she says. "I'm actually late for rehearsal. We might have a really cool gig coming up next month."

"That's awesome. Go to rehearsal! I'm all good here, I promise."

"You sure?"

"Of course I'm sure. Any chance you can come to Jensen's later? Around seven?"

"Sure."

"So we're good?"

"We'll see," Nina says. But she's smiling as she says it.

I give her a quick hug before anyone can notice.

Nina looks me over. "I'm glad you texted." She pauses. "Is something wrong? Or did you just want to see me?"

I wait for a few seconds, trying to decide how to answer.

"Both," I say finally.

21

"Are you guys over your fight?" Eric asks.

I'm sitting at Jensen's with Eric and Jamie, having omelets and fries.

"You mean with Nina?"

Eric rolls his eyes. "No, with Rihanna."

"HA!" cackles Jamie.

"I'm not sure it was a fight, exactly," I say. "More like an intense conversation. And yes, we're over it."

Eric looks slightly disappointed, but he tries to hide it. "Good stuff!"

"So, what happened at the game today?" Jamie asks. "You get into it with Ron?"

"Nah," I say. "Just the usual."

"It looked like you guys were going at it pretty good. Coach too. And then you got benched."

"We were way ahead."

Eric lets out an annoyed little laugh. "Dude. We're your friends. Your best friends, I thought."

"And you and me have been playing football together since before we could walk," Jamie adds.

Eric challenges me with his eyes. "So what gives?"

I'm just about to tell them what happened when Nina gets there. I immediately tense up. "I know I'm a little early," she says. "You guys in the middle of something? I can come back."

"Kinda," Eric says.

"Okay, cool," Nina says. She starts to walk away, but something about that just feels wrong to me, so I get up and grab her arm. "No, stay. Hang with us. I was just telling them about what happened at the game."

Nina sighs. "Football? Again?"

"We like football," Jamie says. "So sue us."

"Easy, bud," I tell him.

Eric stands up. "Actually, I just remembered I have to go."

Jamie takes the cue and also gets up. "Yeah, same."

"Wait, what?" I say.

Eric turns halfway around—not quite enough to look at me. "Yeah, no, it's all good."

"Are you guys for real? I'm sitting here making sure we

get to hang for a while before Nina gets here, and then she gets here ten minutes early and you decide to take off? That's bull."

"So glad you cleared a few minutes in your busy schedule for us, dude," Jamie says. "We know you got a lot going on, it's cool, we don't want to be in the way or anything."

I throw up my hands. "Okay, fine. Like it's my fault I'm starting QB on varsity. So sorry it takes up a lot of time. Whatever. Later."

"Yeah, later," Eric says. Jamie just nods, and they walk away. Nina and I sit quietly for about a minute. I wave to some other kids. Nina looks at the menu, just for something to do.

"Do you need to go make that right?" she asks, finally.

"Nah, it's fine. We'll figure it out."

"Okay, then I'll change the subject," she says. "I'll even change it back to football. Can you tell *me* what happened at the game?"

"Yeah, fine." I actually think it might help to talk about it. "Kenny got hurt on this one play, pretty bad. I don't know if the crowd could tell what was going on, but I was pretty sure he got, like, a concussion. But he didn't want to tell anyone that he was hurt because he didn't want to look like he was being soft."

"Man, what a great game," Nina says, bitterly.

"Then Ron and I got into it a little bit," I go on.

"Love Ron." Nina's on a sarcastic roll.

"Yeah, well, he's the captain, and in case you haven't noticed, he doesn't like me very much. He wanted Kenny to stay in the game, but I told Kenny he had to go out. I told the Coach, too, and I called a different play without telling the coach, to protect Kenny. So yeah, I got in trouble."

Nina stares at me.

"But you know, like I said, I was helping Kenny," I add, trying to get her on my side.

"You made sure a teammate who was hurt didn't keep playing," she says. "That's a step in the right direction, Caleb, but I don't think you deserve a medal or anything."

"I'm not saying I deserve a medal. I just want you to know that I'm hearing what you're saying, and I'm taking the safety of the game seriously."

She looks at me for a long second, then her eyes soften. "And they say jocks are all muscle and no heart."

I feel a surge of warmth through my body. "I'm at least thirty-eight percent heart."

Nina laughs and puts her hand on mine. "Am I being a big nightmare about this?"

I laugh, mostly out of relief that she's not going to yell at me anymore. "You are, kinda, actually."

"I don't mean to be. And I'm sorry."

"About what?"

She takes a sip of my milkshake. "I know how much football means to you and your family. I don't want to take that away from you. All I can ask is that you think about it, about what the dangers are, and as long as you play, be incredibly careful. Or, as careful as you can be."

"I am careful."

"And don't try to stay in a game just to be a tough guy macho man, like your pal Kenny."

"I won't. I swear."

I sit there quietly for a few seconds, just soaking up the fact that she's not telling me to quit football.

"Thanks again for coming to the game, even if you missed me play," I say.

She shrugs. "No biggie. I mean, you came to my concert, remember? It's only fair that I show up."

I finish off my shake. "Yeah, I guess."

She smiles. "I actually did get there in time to see you play for a few minutes, before you came out. I enjoyed it. I didn't want to, but I did. You're so damn good at that idiotic game."

"Thanks, I guess."

We're officially over our first fight when she leans over the table and kisses me. For more than a few seconds.

I can see Eric and Jamie, at another table, looking at us.

So I close my eyes.

22

The first thing you realize when you're shooting a commercial is that the lights are hot.

Really hot.

The second thing is that there are a lot of people working on the commercial, but as far as I can tell, they spend most of their time eating cookies at the food table.

My dad and I are standing there in his showroom, with two sweet-looking cars behind us. The director, a no-nonsense woman with spiky hair named Ruby, is telling us what to do.

"Now, Dad, you're gonna stand here next to the one car, and you're gonna say 'My car's a classic!' and then Caleb, you're gonna enter the frame and stand next to the other car and say, 'Yeah, Dad, but mine's the hottest new model, and sometimes you have to make room for the new guy!' And then you wink at Dad, and Dad says, 'Dang it, not again!' And that's when we're going to cut to footage with the narrator talking about the best new and used car collections in the whole state. You guys got it? Any questions?"

My dad raises his hand, like he's a fourth grader in school. "Uh, yeah . . . why are you calling me Dad?"

Ruby blinks a few times. "Uh, well, I'm sorry, Mr. Springer, no real reason. You're the dad in the commercial, and so I guess maybe that's why. Anyway, are we ready to get started?"

My dad takes his place in front of his car, and Ruby barks out some instructions to the crew, who finish their snacks and take their positions. Then she yells, "ACTION!"

My dad looks into the camera with his million-dollar smile. "My car's a classic!"

I run out in front of my car. "Yeah, Dad, but mine's the hottest new model, and sometimes you have to make room for the new guy!"

I wink at Dad, he winks back, and I wait for him to say his line. But he doesn't. He doesn't say anything, in fact. The only thing that happens is that his million-dollar smile disappears.

After a few seconds, Ruby yells, "CUT!" She hurries over to my dad. "Everything okay, Mr. Springer?"

"Call me Sammy," he says, quietly.

"Sorry, Sammy . . . everything okay?"

"Yeah, everything's great. Just forgot what I'm supposed to say, that's all."

" 'Dang it, not again!' "

"What? That was only the first take!"

Ruby lets out a loud laugh, then immediately realizes my dad's not kidding. "No, no, Sammy . . . that's the line. 'Dang it, not again!' "

"Oh!" Now my dad laughs. "Haha, yeah, that's funny!"

"Should we give it a go?" Ruby asks, gently.

My dad nods forcefully, trying to look confident. "Yeah, yeah, let's try this thing again."

I glance over at my mom, who's standing behind the camera, watching. She smiles and gives me a thumbs-up. Then she mouths something to me, but I don't understand, so she does it again, more slowly.

This time I get it.

Keep an eye on your dad.

We go through the routine again—my dad says his line, I say my line, I wink, and this time my dad says, "Whoa, the new guy! What's up?"

"CUT!" yells Ruby.

My dad smacks his forehead and says, "Damn! My bad! I got this!"

But he doesn't have it. We try about ten more times, but my dad gets something wrong every time, either the second line or the first line, or he forgets to wink, or he starts talking before I finish talking—if there's a way to mess it up, he messes it up. But that's not the worst part. The worst part is he keeps getting madder and madder at himself about it.

Finally, after one last mistake, my dad yells, "THAT'S IT! I SUCK! I'M OUT!" and storms off the set.

No one moves except my mom, who runs after him. The crew, the camera people, and I all wait for Ruby to tell us what to do. Finally, she says, "That's a wrap, everyone."

It's only when everyone starts packing up their stuff that I realize that's commercial-speak for, "We're done here."

⁂

A few minutes later, we're standing in the parking lot, and my dad is saying, "Dang it, not again!" over and over.

I give him a hug and try to break the tension. "Nailed it, Dad! A little late, but nailed it."

It works. He laughs. "Yeah, right? I'm gonna need to pay all those people to come back another day, that's what kills me." Then he smacks my shoulder. "You were great, by the way. If this whole quarterbacking thing doesn't work out, you could be in the movies!"

"Hey," says my mom. "What do you actors say we go get some brunch at Rawley's? May as well make the most of the day, right?"

I'm fully on board with that idea. Rawley's has these chocolate chip pancakes that will fix anything—for an hour, anyway.

We get there, and immediately five people come over to my dad to shake his hand. He's incredibly sweet with all of them—sharp, funny, friendly. That's the thing that's so hard to understand. Whatever's going on in his head seems to come and go in a matter of seconds.

The waiter comes over to take our order.

"I'll have the eggs over easy with sausage and wheat toast," says my dad. "And the strawberry pancakes, the French toast, a cheeseburger deluxe, a spinach and cheddar omelet, a chocolate shake, and a chicken noodle soup."

The waiter glances over at my mother. "You got more folks coming?"

My mom shakes her head. "Nope," she says. "My husband is just extremely hungry." I don't need to look at her to know what she's thinking. She's not going to ask my dad why he just ordered the whole left side of the menu. This is one conversation not worth having.

At the end of brunch, my mom packs up all the extra food and puts it in the trunk. She'll drop it off at the food pantry later. When we get home, I tell my parents that I'm going over to Nina's house to do homework.

My dad looks at me, winks, and says, "Dang it, not again!"

Walthorne High vs. Ramsdale High
Season Record: 10–0
State Semifinal

WWHS
WALTHORNE HIGH SCHOOL RADIO
TRANSCRIPT OF PLAY-BY-PLAY
ALFIE JENKS AND JULIAN HESS

ALFIE: Well, there's no doubt that Walthorne faces its toughest test of the season tonight, as the Wildcats take on the 8–2 New Bradford Titans in the state semifinal. New Bradford is led by their six-foot, four-inch, 305-pound defensive end, Marcus Wingfield, who has racked up seventeen sacks on the season. He'll be trying to chase down Caleb Springer, Walthorne's sensational quarterback, who's looking to break single-season passing records in completions, touchdowns, and total yards—as a freshman! There's a great crowd on hand, and they should be in for a treat . . .

⁜⁜⁜

Buck works overtime tonight.

If it weren't for him, I'd probably be dead and buried about now.

The first time I get popped is halfway through the first quarter, when New Bradford's ginormous defensive end closes down on me like an angry bear. I manage to sidestep him, but unfortunately I run right into the linebacker from the other side, who's not quite as big but still hits plenty hard.

He cracks me shoulder to shoulder, a perfectly legal hit, but I don't have time to brace myself, and my head hits the turf with a *CRUNK!*

I feel it—oh yeah, I feel it—but I pop up. I'm fine.

In the huddle, I say to Ron, "Hey, what do you say we try to prevent these guys from knocking the living crap out of me?"

He growls at me. "What do you think we're doing out here, having a tea party?"

"Hard to tell, to be honest," I say.

"Go eff yourself."

"Happy to, as long as you block for me."

We've reached the point in the season where who's a senior and who's a freshman doesn't really matter anymore. We've been through the wars together. No one's better than anyone else, and no one person can do it alone—it's everyone or no one. We don't have to like one another; we just have to look out for one another.

On the next play, Ron levels the giant dude, and Ethan Metzger catches a slant for eighteen yards.

⁂

ALFIE: Two minutes to go in the first half, and Walthorne is trying to build on their 14–6 lead. It's third and nine at the New Bradford seventeen yard line, which is definitely a passing situation. Springer is in the shotgun, he takes the snap and drifts out to his right . . . The protection is good, Springer looks downfield, no one open . . . He cuts back upfield and decides to take it himself. Oh, the coaches have to be holding their breath here . . . Springer is at the first down marker, he goes into the protective slide . . . but oh! He's popped by Wingfield! The all-state D-lineman comes in late and practically rips Springer's head off!

Ron Johnson runs over to protect his quarterback . . . Now there's a scuffle!

JULIAN: Oh, you don't like to see this, Alfie, but sometimes it's unavoidable, with emotions running so high . . .

ALFIE: That's right, Julian. This is a physical game and sometimes these guys are gonna get into some extracurricular activity . . .

JULIAN: Excellent metaphor there, Alfie. My English teacher, Ms. Priore, would be very proud.

ALFIE: Thank you, Julian.

JULIAN: Oh boy, check this out!

ALFIE: Ron Johnson and Marcus Wingfield are now pushing and shoving each other, the two biggest guys on the field! The crowd is screaming, loving it, but this could get ugly! The refs run over, coaches are on the field . . . Now it seems to be settling down . . . Both players head to their respective sidelines . . . Definite unsportsmanlike penalties on Johnson and Wingfield . . . Meanwhile, Springer took quite a shot on that play, but he seems to be fine . . .

⁜ ⁜ ⁜

We end up scoring on the drive, and at the half we're up 21–6. On the way to the locker room, I see my dad sprinting down the sideline. He usually doesn't talk to anyone until after the game, so I brace myself for something I must have done really wrong. But he's not heading for me, he's heading for the referee, and as soon as he gets there, he starts screaming.

"WHY WASN'T THAT KID TOSSED?! THAT'S BULLSHIT, FRED, AND YOU KNOW IT! HE SHOULD BE GONE!"

The ref, whose name is Fred, I guess, gets right back in my dad's face. "You don't know what you're talking about, Sammy! Get out of here before I throw your ass out!"

The two keep going at it for a few minutes, and I'm getting ready for my dad to get tossed, but from one second to the next he stops yelling and gives the ref a big hug. "You're doing an amazing job, Freddy. Keep up the good work! Say hi to Angela and the kids for me."

My dad walks away without even looking in my direction. I catch the ref's eye and shrug.

The ref gives me a short nod. "Your dad's a freakin' legend. Love that guy."

I walk to the locker room, shaking my head. Only my dad could bite a ref's head off and then be called a "freakin' legend" two seconds later by the same guy.

⁘⁘⁘

ALFIE:	Well, the second half has been all Walthorne, and with five minutes to go in the fourth quarter and the score 45–17, the Wildcats take over on downs at their own forty-seven yard line.
JULIAN:	I'm a little surprised that Coach Toffler still has his first team in, but this will probably be their last drive. I'm sure they'll keep the ball on the ground, trying to eat some clock as this game winds down. Coach will want to get his starters some rest before the championship game next Friday night.

ALFIE: Excellent point, Julian.

JULIAN: Wait, seriously?

ALFIE: Yes, seriously.

JULIAN: Alfie complimented me! It's official! I rock! I totally rock!

ALFIE: Easy, Julian. It's first and ten . . . Oh, look at this: Springer is dropping back to pass. This is a surprise! Protection is good, no one open downfield, Springer starts to scramble . . . and he's taken down by Wingfield. Looks like Springer landed hard on his shoulder, his right shoulder, his throwing arm . . . You don't want to mess with that . . . Yup, sure enough, Coach is motioning Springer to the sidelines. He's done for the night.

JULIAN: He did his job, though, throwing for well over two hundred yards and three touchdowns . . . This freshman never fails to impress, and the larger the expectations, the better he performs . . .

⁂

I'm not positive, but I'm pretty sure the big guy turns his body just so he can slam his entire weight down on top of me as my right shoulder mashes into the ground.

But that's what shoulder pads are for, right? I never gave my shoulder pads a name; maybe I should.

I'm fine, though, and two of my linemen help me up. We're heading back to the huddle when Coach Toffler starts waving his arms wildly over his head. He wants me to come out. My instinct is to protest, to ask to stay in the game, but I know that's not going to work. I slap hands with my replacement QB, Arch Daniels, and run over to the coach.

"Should have thrown that one away to avoid the sack," he says. "Take a seat."

Would it kill you to say I played a good game? I want to ask him, but don't.

We end up winning 45–25, meaning we made it to the finals, but when we huddle up after the game, Ron tells us not to celebrate. "This isn't what we came for. This is nothing. NOTHING! We're NOWHERE! We haven't done ANYTHING!

We don't gloat, we don't strut, we don't preen, we don't party, we don't SMILE! We get back to WORK! We start thinking about tomorrow, and the next day, and the next day, and we FOCUS! We got ONE MORE GAME!"

Everyone screams, "ONE MORE GAME!"

Ron looks at me and winks. The guy has made my life kind of miserable, but I gotta admit, he knows how to get the guys fired up.

We're walking back to the locker room when I hear a voice behind me. A voice I know very well.

My dad's voice.

"Billy! Billy! BILLY!"

Billy is Coach Toffler's first name.

I turn around and see my dad running, just like he did at halftime. I guess his days of waiting for everyone to come to him are over. My mom is right behind him. A crowd is starting to gather in anticipation.

He pokes a finger into Coach's chest. "What are you doing, Billy? You trying to get my kid killed out there?"

"Listen, Sammy, that was gonna be his last series—"

"Last series, BULLSHIT!"

I realize where the expression "spitting mad" comes from, because my dad is spraying as much as he's yelling.

"You're playing with his future! My kid has a million-dollar right arm and you're out there messing around!" Except he doesn't say "messing." He says something way worse.

I sprint over and try to help. "Dad! Dad! It's all good! Remember last game, you were mad because he took me out early? So this time I stayed in the game! But I was always coming out in the fourth quarter!"

But my dad is so focused on the coach, it's like he doesn't even realize I'm there. "This is a once-in-a-lifetime talent, Billy! He's already being recruited at State! We're getting letters every day! This kid is special and you're trying to get him killed out there! You guys were up by thirty! I'm going to be talking to the director of athletics about this!"

My mom is pulling at my dad, but he just keeps saying, "Not now, not now!"

Coach Toffler catches my eye quickly and makes a face, like, *Help me out here, kid.* I realize that my dad isn't doing anybody any favors, especially me, by throwing a tantrum at the coach. So I try again.

"Dad! You know how you're always saying that the worst thing about high school sports is the know-it-all parents who think they're smarter than the coach, and who get in the coach's face telling him what to do, and how obnoxious that is, because all these parents don't know what they're doing and only care about their own kids?"

I glance up and see a bunch of those parents I'm talking about, now with weird looks on their faces, but I don't care. This is more important. "And remember how you said if you ever become one of those nightmare parents that I should tell you to knock it off? Well, I'm telling you now. Knock it off!"

It seems like I'm getting through to him, because he stops yelling for a second. I take the opportunity to repeat myself, but ten times louder. "KNOCK IT OFF, DAD!!!"

The whole place hears that, and everyone and everything gets quiet. The only thing you can hear is the AV crew packing up their equipment.

My dad blinks a few times, like he's just waking up after having been hypnotized, then takes a few steps backward. "Billy, I . . . Yeah, listen, let's forget it. Forget it. I'm sorry I yelled. I just don't want to see my kid get hurt, that's all. You're doing a great job. Good luck next week in the championship."

Coach Toffler's face softens in relief. "No, no, Sammy, I get it. I totally get it. We all remember what happened a few years ago with that freshman kid, Teddy Youngblood. You have to know, my only goal out there is to protect these kids and keep them safe, you know? Everything else is secondary, doesn't matter. You have to know that."

I exchange glances with Kenny, who's dressed in street clothes, still out with that concussion he got. We both know that's not exactly true, but this is not the time to say that out loud.

"Right, right," my dad says. "All good." He walks over to me and puts his hand on my shoulder. "You're okay? Nothing hurts?"

"All good," I tell him. "Nothing hurts. Clean hit."

"Great. I'll meet you at the car."

And just like that, he turns and walks back up to the parking lot. My mom leans into the coach and says something I can't hear, probably an apology, and hurries after my dad. Everyone else is still standing there, processing what just happened, trying to figure out how many seconds have to go by before they can start gossiping about it.

I start walking into the locker room. I feel somebody next to me, and turn to see Ron, walking and shaking his head.

"Man, your dad is so HARDCORE," he says. "And hey—sorry I missed that block that got you popped. I guess when you think about it, this whole damn thing is my fault!" He smacks my shoulder pads and starts laughing. "See you in there, my brother!"

As I walk into the locker room, a feeling hits me. A feeling I've never had before.

I can't wait for the season to be over.

WALTHORNENEWS.COM

WELCOME TO THE JUNGLE

A HIGH SCHOOL SPORTS BLOG ABOUT
THE WALTHORNE WILDCATS

BY ALFIE JENKS

MONDAY, NOVEMBER 14

High School Concussion Report Provokes Questions, Concerns

As the football season winds down, with the undefeated Walthorne Wildcats getting ready to play in the state championship game this Friday night, a new report that highlights the growing number of concussions in high school football is throwing a bit of cold water on what should be a glorious time for the sport, especially here in Walthorne.

According to the *New York Times*, a study by *The Pediatrics Review*, a well-known pediatric medicine magazine, has determined that while overall concussions have gone down—because the number of participants in high school football has also gone down—the percentage of active players getting concussions has increased significantly over the last ten years.

The authors of the study have called for stricter state laws that govern when athletes can return to play after a concussion. They also called on pediatricians to help educate families. "The medical community should ensure that young athletes and their families are aware of the concussion risk associated with their sports of interest," the authors wrote. "Further, pediatricians working with youth sports organizations should advocate the use of safety measures to help prevent serious injury, especially brain injuries."

Head Coach William Toffler of Walthorne High applauded the release of the report. “This is exactly in line with what we are doing, in terms of increased vigilance around these kinds of injuries,” he said in a prepared statement. “Everything we do in our program, from practice protocols to updated equipment, is designed to protect our student-athletes, and we are committed and dedicated to safety above all else.”

5:32 PM
Alfie

hi alfie this is nina rojas

hi nina!

what's up

i saw that article you posted

the concussion one?

yeah

that was a little scary

i know

are people worried?

i don't think too much

the program is paying close attention to it

are they for real tho?

as far as i can tell, yeah

they seem pretty on top of it in terms of making sure kids come out of games if they seem hurt

okay. caleb told me this kid got hurt

and he stayed in . . .

he says that's just how it is in football

it used to be but not anymore i don't think

but thanks for telling me

i'll check it out

thx!

caleb is so awesome though

he's going pro for sure

yeah i know he's great

but i don't like football

it scares me

i think he could get hurt

yeah true

but his dad was like a pro football player

so it's not like he has a choice

plus he's amazing so there's that

lol i guess

i just don't get how people can love something so much

when it's so dangerous and people get hurt all the time

because that's how people are

i mean i love it

does that make me a bad person??

hahaha of course not.

phew ☺

how are you?

still doing that band thing?

yup i am

it's good thx

cool

you guys were so good at grandage hall

are you playing again soon?

hopefully

we have a gig coming up soon somewhere else actually

cool

i totally want to come if i can!

good luck!
thx
👍👍

23

We're hanging out at Nina's favorite smoothie place. I'm not a big smoothie guy, so I'm sipping on an iced tea and trying to do homework. Nina's working on song lyrics, but she won't show them to me. She never shows them to me until they're done.

We don't talk much, but it's cool. We're at that place in our relationship where we can just be chill around each other and still be glad we're together.

The championship game is in three days and I'm at the point where I just want to focus on the game. I don't really want to talk to anybody outside of my team, my family, or Nina. There's the game, and nothing else exists. That's pretty much how everyone else feels, too, including whoever owns this smoothie shop. Whenever I get tired of staring at my laptop, I can look up at the giant sign in the window that says GO 'CATS! BEAT DEAVER! The whole town is in it together. As my dad says, *It's more than just a football game. It's life itself.*

After a while, Nina stops typing and says, "Desert Island?"

I smile. "Sure. Any excuse to stop doing biology."

Desert Island is a game we play sometimes, where we talk about the things we would want if we lived on a faraway island somewhere. It's a silly way to pass the time, but it's also nice to think about escaping to a place where no one could find us. If only for a little while.

"Your one food," she says.

"That's easy. Scrambled eggs and toast."

"That's two foods."

"Fine, forget the toast. How about you?"

"Duh. Smoothies."

"I think technically that's, like, five foods."

"No way."

"Yes way. Fruit and milk and yogurt and a bunch of other stuff."

She punches me, lightly.

I ask her, "Your one song?"

" 'Taxman,' by the Beatles," she says instantly. "You?"

" 'The Only Place,' by Nina Rojas."

"Cut it out."

"I'm serious."

I've never seen Nina blush until this moment. And boy, does she blush. But it's a happy blush.

"That reminds me," she says. "I can't remember if I told you, but I might have to miss your game. At least part of it."

My mood suddenly shifts. "Wait, what? What do you mean?"

"Brian got a text last night from that coffee bar in Trafford. You know, the one I told you about?"

"You didn't tell me about any coffee bar in Trafford."

"I didn't? Dang, I meant to. It's this really cool place, and some awesome people played there before they were famous, like Tracy Chapman and Michelle Shocked and artists like that."

"I don't know who those people are."

Nina rolls her eyes impatiently. "It doesn't matter. It's kind of a massive honor to land a gig there, especially at our age, but Brian's brother knows the cousin of one of the guys who runs it, and I guess they asked if we wanted to open the show on Friday night."

"Open?"

"Yeah, you know, play before the featured band, like just to get the crowd warmed up and stuff."

"Who's the other band? Are they famous?"

"I have no idea. What's with all the questions? Isn't this awesome?"

"Oh yeah, totally." But the truth is, I'm not really thinking about how awesome it is. I'm thinking that Nina might miss me win the state championship.

She knows exactly what I'm thinking, of course.

"I'm sorry, Caleb. I know it's sucky timing."

I shake my head, determined not to let my disappointment show. "No, it's cool, it's a great opportunity for you. You're gonna kill it. And one day soon, someone's going to open for you guys."

We're both silent for a few seconds, then Nina says, "I hope I didn't just bum you out."

"Yeah, no, you didn't. I'm just kind of, you know, I just want the game to freakin' get here at this point."

"Try to enjoy it, Caleb. You're gonna kill it, too!"

I laugh. "So it's official: We're both gonna kill it on Friday night."

"Yup."

We both take sips of our drinks.

"Your one movie?" Nina asks.

"*Goodfellas.*"

"Mine too!"

We look at each other and smile. Then we open our laptops and get back to work.

The desert island will have to wait.

24

The funny thing is, we've played ten games, but my body hurts less this week than it has all season.

That's because Coach has decided that we're not going to do any real hitting or running in practice. It's like all of a sudden he realized we're actual human beings, and he doesn't want anyone getting hurt before the big game. Or maybe the article about concussions that Alfie wrote got him spooked. Whatever the reason, during practice we mostly just walk through plays, watch film of Deaver's games, talk about our game plan, and listen to the coaches give us motivational speeches about how this game will be one of the most important moments in our lives, and if we win, we will be state champions, and no one will be able to take that away from us for as long as we live.

All I know is, we don't have to run suicide sprints. We've been dealing with those nightmares every day since August 1.

So with my body feeling good, falling asleep is easy. Which is why I'm snoring away when I feel a tug on my shoulder.

I open one eye and can barely make out my mom standing there. “Ma?” I say. “What time is it?”

“Twelve thirty.”

I force myself up on one elbow. “Like, twelve thirty at night? What—what’s happening?”

Before she can speak, though, I know what she’s going to say. I’m still three-quarters asleep, but I know.

“It’s your dad.”

“What about him?”

I see her move, and suddenly the light in my bedroom is on. It’s blinding. I can see my mom is already dressed.

“We need to go.”

⁂

As I’m getting dressed, my mom tells me what happened. She and my dad were watching TV before bed, just like always. Then my dad jumps up and says he needs to drive down to the dealership to get some papers he left there. Before my mom can stop him, he’s out the door and in the car. She waits fifteen minutes, a half an hour, forty-five minutes . . . Finally, after an hour, she starts calling his cell phone. No answer. She tries again.

No answer. She drives down to the dealership and there's no sign that he went into his office at all. She drives home in a panic and calls the police.

I interrupt to ask, "And I'm just sleeping this whole time? Why didn't you wake me up?"

"I didn't want to," she says, "until I knew what was happening."

Finally, just after midnight, the police call and say they found him, and can she come back down to the dealership.

So that's where we're heading now.

In the car, neither one of us speaks for the first five minutes. Then my mom turns off the radio, which means she wants to say something.

I wait.

After a few more seconds, she takes a big breath, then says, "I've been begging him to see a doctor."

I stare at her. "You have?"

Her hands grip the wheel tightly. "Yeah. For the last couple of months, since it became clear what was going on. I didn't want to tell you. I didn't want to worry you."

"And he said no?"

She glances over at me. "Have you met your father?"

I don't answer.

She puts the radio back on—classic soft rock, which she loves. Usually, she sings along. Tonight, she doesn't.

We see the lights of the dealership up ahead. The red and blue lights of police cars spin and flash, too. It feels like we're driving onto a movie set. But we're not.

As we get out of the car, a woman in a suit walks up to us. "Ms. Springer?"

"Yes?"

"I'm Detective Abosa. Please come this way." The detective spots me. "This your son?"

"Our son, Caleb, yes."

"Ah, the QB. Nice to meet you, Caleb. Sorry to get you out here so late, especially during championship week."

Man, even the cops are all about it. "It's no problem," I say. "Are you taking us to my dad?"

"I am."

We head around the side of the building, where all the cars for sale are in a giant lot. A small crowd is gathered by the SUVs.

I assume they're all police. They're looking up at something, shining their flashlights, and it takes me a few seconds to figure out what it is. Then I see it.

Or, I should say, then I see *him.*

My dad.

I have no idea what he could possibly be doing until I realize he has a pillow and blanket with him.

He decided to spend the night sleeping on the roof of a brand-new car.

"One of our patrolmen spotted him about a half hour ago," Detective Abosa tells my mom. "We've been trying to get your husband down, but he doesn't seem interested. We thought you might have better luck."

My mom starts to run toward him. "Sam? Sammy?"

My dad lifts his head, stretches, gives my mom a big smile. "Honey! What are you doing here?" His voice is weird and distant, like he's talking in his sleep.

My mom hesitates for a second, then says, "Well, I could ask you the same question."

"I'm getting some rest," my dad says. "Or I was until these people woke me up."

"Okay," my mom says. "But why are you sleeping here?"

My dad hesitates, like he's deciding if that's the dumbest question in the world or the smartest question in the world. Either way, he doesn't answer. Instead, he looks at me and says, "Caleb."

It's hard for me to look at him, because the lights are so bright, and also, because it just is.

"Hey, Dad."

"Big game coming up."

"I know, Dad."

"Sammy?" My mom's tone is different this time. More urgent. "Sammy, please. Come down from there. We need to go home."

My dad lies back down. "I'm tired. I need to go to sleep."

The detective walks over to my mom. "We could get a doctor or a therapist or someone down here if you think it might help—"

But my mom shakes her head. "SAM!" she shouts, so loud that the other cops stop chatting. "Come down now! Caleb needs to get some rest, too! It's championship week! So come on down! NOW! Otherwise Caleb WON'T BE ABLE TO PLAY!"

Well, that does the trick.

My dad stretches and yawns, then leaps down off the car. Watching him do it so gracefully reminds me what a great athlete he still is.

He's got the pillow in his hand. My mom takes it from him. I recognize it—it's from our guest room. The blanket is, too. He must have taken them when he left the house earlier.

My dad still doesn't look fully awake, but I recognize the confused look on his face, because I've been seeing it more and more often over the past few months. Detective Abosa whispers something to my mom and hands her a card. My mom puts the card in her jacket pocket, then grabs my dad's hand.

"Let's go home," my mom says, softly. "Whaddya say, honey? You want to go home?"

My dad doesn't answer for a few seconds as he watches the various cops start to pack up their stuff. Finally, he answers my mom, but this time his voice is different. Wide awake. Normal.

"I thought I *was* home," he says.

PART III
Sun

25

When my mom announces at breakfast the next morning that she made an appointment with Dr. Lucci, who she says comes recommended by everyone, my dad doesn't even look up from his grapefruit.

"Have fun. I'm not going."

My mom looks exhausted but determined. "We talked about this. You agreed. And Caleb is coming with us."

"Last night was some weird sleepwalking thing," my dad says. "Or maybe it was my pain meds. My back has been killing me lately." That's another fun part of being an ex-NFL player—he's got aches and pains all over his body—back, legs, shoulders, ankles. He used to take a lot of pain medication, before my mom helped him give them up.

"You're back on the meds?" my mom asks. "Let me see them. Get them for me."

My dad stares straight ahead.

"I didn't think so. Appointment is tomorrow at ten thirty."

"I said I'm not going."

My mom gets up and pours herself some more coffee. She paces around the kitchen. I pretend to busy myself with homework.

Finally, she says, "You're going to that doctor's appointment or I'm done. I mean it."

It's like all the air goes out of the room. My mom stands at the kitchen sink, not taking her eyes off my dad. I look across at him, and I can see his jaw muscle pumping, almost beating, like a heart, but his mouth isn't open. His neck is getting red, which happens when he gets worked up. I try to prepare myself for the yell I think is coming—even though when he really gets going, nothing can prepare you for that.

A few more moments of dead silence.

Then he does say something. But it's not a yell. In fact, it's so soft, you can barely hear it.

And it's only one word.

"Fine."

⁂

Dr. Lucci is a neurologist. A brain doctor. Her office is really fancy—she must be good at her job. We meet her, say hello, and then she takes my dad away for some tests. My mom and I sit in the office for a few minutes, not doing much of anything, then she says, "Want to go get ice cream?"

I laugh a little. "It's eleven in the morning."

"That's okay. I bet they're open."

Well, you don't have to ask me twice. Fifteen minutes later we're sitting at Dusty's and I'm holding a coffee shake. My mom orders a child-sized chocolate dip cone, her favorite.

I slurp a sip. "Don't tell Coach," I say. "Or Dad."

"I won't," Mom says with a laugh.

We're quiet for about a minute, then my mom says, "You're it, you know."

I'm not sure what she means, but I don't say anything. I figure she'll explain. And she does.

"You're what's keeping him going. You and football and watching you become what you are. It gives him so much joy." She pauses for a few seconds, then adds, "It's one of the only things that gives him joy."

I keep sipping my shake.

"But it also gives me joy," she adds. "And makes me so proud. I worry, yes, but I love watching you play and shine and be the best, and making Dad happy. I love it. And it's possible that I love it a little too much, if you know what I mean."

My mom sits back in her chair. A lot of things are running through my head—the pressure of playing, the danger of playing, the thrill of playing, the possibility of not playing. But the only thing that comes out of my mouth is, "I do know what you mean."

She gives me a tired smile. "You know how much we love you, right, Caleb?"

"Of course I do, Mom."

"You know we'd do anything for you, right?"

"Yeah."

She's got a tiny smear of chocolate above her lip, and it reminds me that my mom never has a hair, or anything else, out of place. She's the most put-together person I've ever seen, at least on the outside. Inside might be a different story.

"I'm glad you know that," she says. "We'd do anything for you. But that doesn't mean . . . that doesn't mean you have to do everything for us."

I feel my heart thump a little in my chest. "What do you mean, Mom?"

She takes a napkin and wipes the smear away, and just like that she's perfect again. "I mean, there are going to be some tough times ahead, for all of us. And you're going to have some decisions to make, and they're not going to be easy. But they're your decisions. If you want to talk about anything, or want my opinion on anything, I'm always here for you. I hope you know that."

I stare down into my shake, because I don't want her to see me almost cry. I haven't said anything to her about how I'm feeling about football, how confused about it I am, but it turns out I don't have to. She gets it. She gets everything.

That's how moms work, I guess.

"Thanks," I manage to croak out. "I might."

"Okay, honey."

Her phone buzzes, and we both jump a little, jolted back to the immediate situation. She looks down and reads a text.

"They're ready," she says.

26

Dr. Lucci gets right to the point.

"Your husband is showing symptoms of what is called early-onset dementia," she tells my mom, as if my dad isn't sitting right there. "It's very uncommon at his age, but I know Samuel played professional football, and there is certainly a growing amount of evidence that the trauma caused by repeated blows to the head can be an underlying cause."

So there it is. My dad is sick. Football causes brain damage.

My dad is sick because he played football.

The room is silent for a few seconds as the doctor lets us absorb that news. I have a zillion things going through my head. That my dad is going to be different for the rest of his life. That his strange behavior is going to continue, and probably get worse. That his sickness is almost definitely a result of playing this game that he and I both love so much. This game that I'm so good at, that could open up the world for me.

Like my mom said—I have some tough decisions to make.

I see her grab my dad's hand.

"From what I understand," the doctor continues, "Samuel has been aware of his condition for some time but has done his best to conceal it from his family."

My mom gives a tiny shake of her head. "I knew," she says. "I didn't want to admit it to myself, but I knew."

"I knew, too," I say, barely louder than a whisper.

My dad turns to me. There are tears in his eyes. "This is on me. I refused to talk about it. I thought if I ignored it, I could make it go away, make it not real. It took me a long time to admit it to Mom, but I knew she knew. I knew I would have to deal with it. I just didn't think it would be this soon. But you, Caleb . . . I was . . . I couldn't. I'm sorry, son."

I get out of my chair and hug my dad. "It's okay, Dad. Seriously. I get it. It's okay."

He hugs me back. "You're the football player in the family now, son, and it's a much safer game now. You make me so proud every time you go out onto that field. I see what I used to be, and that makes all this a little easier to take."

I try to push all the doubts about football out of my mind, just for the moment. "I'm glad, Dad," I tell him. "I'm glad."

My dad is still holding on to me, so I don't move. Nobody talks for a minute, then Dr. Lucci says, "I don't want to sugarcoat it, because this is not a situation with a miracle cure. There's a lot of great research happening, and some promising developments, but they're still a ways off. In the meantime, we've got all sorts of exercises and activities to help Samuel. There's a lot we can do to make sure he stays healthy and positive, and with his family's support and love, I have no doubt he'll do really well."

I can feel my dad's incredibly strong hands—the hands that made him Sammy "Dinger" Springer, all-pro NFL wide receiver—as they squeeze me tight.

"We're going to fix this, Dad," I say into his chest. "We're going to help you get better."

Nobody says it out loud, but we all know the truth.

With this disease, there's no such thing as getting better.

27

Three hours later I'm in the school gym, trying to smile my way through a giant pep rally.

The whole team is sitting in folding chairs on some type of stage they set up for the occasion. Coach Toffler is introducing the players, one at a time. It takes forever because there are more than forty of us. It's like a graduation, except we're not graduating from anything.

The subs go first, then the starters. First the defense, then the offense.

When Coach introduces the offensive line, Ron Johnson gets the students riled up by flapping his arms up and down like some sort of hyperactive eagle. Kenny, who's recovered from his concussion and back in the starting lineup, slaps hands with me before he goes up onto the stage. "Dude, they're gonna roar for you," he says. They announce the wide receivers, then the running backs.

And just like that, I'm the last guy sitting there.

"And last but certainly not least," Coach Toffler says, his voice starting to rise in volume, "our quarterback, number 12, the man who is going to help us take home the trophy, a once-in-a-generation talent, freshman Caleb Springer."

I get up out of my chair and walk onto the stage. The whole gym is hooting and hollering. Coach shakes my hand, then whispers, "Say a few words. They'd love to hear from you."

I glance back at Ron, who nods at me. He's our captain, and the largest human being in our school, but even he knows that when the time comes, no one wants to hear from the center. They want to hear from the QB.

Me.

Coach hands me the microphone. "Wow," I say, my voice echoing off the walls. "This is really cool. I've never been to one of these before."

Someone yells, "That's because you've never been in high school before!" and everyone laughs.

I laugh, too. "That's true. I don't really have much to say, except I'm really excited for the game tomorrow night, and I hope everyone comes out to watch!"

More cheers. I see a hand go up in front of me—it's Alfie Jenks, wanting to ask a question. I glance over at the coach, and he shrugs. *Sure, why not?*

I nod. "Hey, Alfie, what's up?"

She holds her phone up, and I realize she's recording my answer. "A report just came out about concussions in high school and college football. Did you see my blog post about it?"

"Uh . . . I think I heard something about it."

I see Coach Toffler out of the corner of my eye, shaking his head. He starts walking toward me.

Alfie follows up: "There have been a bunch of articles, like in the *New York Times* and stuff, about concussions and other head injuries in the NFL and college, but now they're starting to look at high school football, too."

"I don't know anything about that—"

"What about your dad?" Alfie asks. "Wasn't he an NF—"

But that's when Coach Toffler reaches me, and he grabs the microphone out of my hand. "Alfie, Alfie!" he says, cutting her off. "What is this, ESPN? You going for a Pulitzer Prize or something? Come on, now. This is a celebration, not an inquisition!" Then he leans into me and whispers, "Go ahead over there and stand with your teammates."

I walk over, with Alfie's questions ringing in my ears. Ron leans in and says, "What is up with HER? That was BULL!"

After another few minutes, the pep rally is over. We're getting off the makeshift stage when I feel someone's hand on my back, and I turn to see Nina. She looks upset.

"You okay?" she asks.

"Yeah, I'm fine."

For a second I think she's going to take me on about it, but she obviously realizes this isn't the time. "I saw that blog post by Alfie, but I didn't think she would bring it up the day before the game. That doesn't seem fair."

"It's nothing," I say, trying to laugh it off. "People need stuff to talk about, write about. It's stupid. I'm good. Seriously!" I see Alfie talking to someone a few feet away and yell, "Hey, Alfie! What was that about? Suddenly you're like trying to be all *60 Minutes* or something? I need to focus on the game!"

"I'm sorry, Caleb," she yells back. "I didn't mean to make you upset. I just wanted to know if you'd heard about that report."

"No, and I don't want to know about it!" I turn back to Nina, desperate to change the subject. "You guys ready for your gig tomorrow night?"

But she doesn't answer. Instead, she says, "At some point, you probably should check it out."

"Check out what?"

"The report, Caleb," Nina says, gently.

I can feel my skin getting hot with irritation, and I lash out. "What happened to not bringing it up the day before the game? And what's it going to tell me anyway, that football is dangerous? Wow. What a fascinating piece of information."

There's a look of concerned surprise on Nina's face. "Whoa. You reminded me of your dad just then." My eyes immediately fill up with tears. Nina notices right away, of course, and her face goes from concern to alarm. "Caleb? Caleb, what is it? What's going on?"

I haven't told her. I haven't told her about my dad sleeping on top of a car, and going to the doctor. And I can't tell her what it feels like right now, to have all the air go out of my lungs, like I can't breathe, after she said I reminded her of my dad. I can't tell her exactly what that means, and how scary it is. I can't tell her any of that.

And then, suddenly, I can. In fact, I have to.

I pull her into a corner, away from everyone and everything.

"My dad . . ." I'm struggling to find the words. "My dad . . . We took him to see a doctor. And . . . And, uh . . . it was . . . His brain is . . . He's . . . uh . . ."

But I don't have to finish the sentence. Nina knows. In fact, she probably knew before me.

She pulls me into a tight hug. "Oh, Caleb, I am sorry. I am so, so sorry."

"Yeah," I say, my head buried in her shoulder. "It's . . . It sucks. It really sucks."

"I know. I know." She pulls back to look me in the eye. "But you guys are an incredible family, and you'll figure this out together."

"Thanks. Yeah, I know we will. It's just that . . . Well, there's a lot to figure out, actually . . . and Alfie bringing up that report doesn't help."

"Forget all that. Seriously, Caleb, don't think about any of that right now."

I let out a long breath and wipe my eyes, trying to get it together. Can't let anyone see the starting quarterback bawling the day before the championship game.

"Do you want me to come over later, and we can hang out?" Nina asks. "Or maybe we can go get pizza?"

I let out a little laugh. “Ha! Can you imagine? Skipping pregame dinner? My dad would just love that.”

“Oh right,” she says. “The intense pregame meal. A family tradition.”

I sigh. “If I had to take a wild guess, I’d say tonight’s meal is going to be even more intense than usual.”

I’m waiting for Nina to ask me how I could still consider playing in a football game right after my dad got diagnosed with dementia, but instead, she puts her hand on my shoulder. “I could come to dinner, if you want—you know, if your parents would be cool with it.”

I blink a few times. “You would do that for me?”

“Of course. Maybe it will help distract you, take some of the pressure off. Maybe it will help you have a great game tomorrow night.”

For a few seconds, I can’t quite believe what I’m hearing. I feel so grateful that this incredible person likes me.

I take her hand off my shoulder and put it in my hand and squeeze hard.

She squeezes it back. “And then after you win the championship,” she says, “you will read that report.”

28

Usually we go to Stokeley's the night before games, but because of what's going on with my dad, we decide to eat at home. My mom ends up cooking an amazing chicken potpie (light on the peas), and my dad gets into the act by making his famous magic bars for dessert. (I'll only eat two—the rest are for after the game.)

A few minutes before dinner, Nina comes over. My mom welcomes her with a bright smile, which is no surprise, since that's the way she is with everyone.

But my dad looks confused. "Wait, I thought we were having our pregame meal. I mean, not at Stokeley's, but everything else the same."

"We are, Dad."

"But we don't usually have company for that."

"I asked Nina to come. It's good; it will help me relax."

My dad doesn't get the concept of relaxing before a game, but he lets it go. Instead, he looks at Nina and says, "I hope you don't mind plenty of football talk. Caleb and I have a lot to cover in terms of strategy for the game."

“I don’t mind,” Nina answers, looking him straight in the eye. “As long as it doesn’t make Caleb too nervous.”

My dad laughs, but not the way you laugh when you think something is funny. “Don’t you worry about that! A few nerves is natural. It’s a good thing.”

The potpie is delicious, and my mom does a pretty good job of steering the conversation, asking Nina about her band (“It’s going great; I have a gig tomorrow night actually”), if she plays any sports (“Not since fifth grade”), and what’s her favorite subject in school (“Depends on the teacher”). My dad eats quietly, minding his own business, trying to stay patient, until finally he can’t take it anymore.

“Caleb and I need to talk about the game.”

“Oh, sorry,” Nina says.

“No, it’s fine, Nina,” my dad says. “And I hope to hear your band play someday. Caleb says you’re terrific.” Amazingly enough, he seems to like her. But then it’s on to business. “So, I looked at some of that game film you sent me, Cae. Their outside linebackers seem vulnerable. I would think some option plays and some quick screens are going to be a big part of the offensive scheme tomorrow night, am I right?”

"I'm not sure, Dad. We've been working on some slants in practice."

My dad shakes his head. "Slants? SLANTS? That plays right into their two inside backers, who are the best athletes on that team! No, no, that's all wrong. That's wrong. I'm going to call the coach."

I sigh, because I really don't feel like going down this road, especially with Nina here to see it.

"Don't call the coach, Dad."

"Why not?"

"Just please don't."

"He loves talking to me."

"He loves talking to you when you're nice, because you're a former NFL star. But he doesn't want parents chirping in his ear about what to do. No coach wants that, Dad, remember?"

My dad sighs gruffly. "Maybe I should coach this team. The only reason you guys are where you are is because you're the quarterback. He should thank his lucky stars that I didn't send you to prep school. I had schools begging me, calling me every day. They wanted to give you a free ride—"

"We've been over this, Dad. I wanted to go to school with my friends—"

My dad slams his hand down on the table. "IT'S NOT ALWAYS ABOUT WHAT YOU WANT THOUGH, IS IT?!"

The volume of his voice blows through the house like a windstorm. Nina literally jumps. The dishes rattle. My mom bows her head as if to pray, but I know she isn't praying. She's just hiding without getting up.

Nobody moves while my dad's breathing returns to normal. Then he says, "My point, Caleb, is that their inside linebackers are much more athletic than their outside linebackers, and so you need to work the corners of the field—"

"I don't think we should talk about football anymore."

My dad stops. He has a look of total confusion on his face, maybe because of who spoke.

It wasn't me. It wasn't my mom.

It was Nina.

My dad gazes across at her. "I'm sorry, what?"

"I don't think we should talk about football anymore," Nina says again. "It just seems to stress everyone out, and I think the important thing to do now is relax." Her voice gets a little sturdier with every word.

My mom grabs my dad's arm. "She's right, honey. Let's find something else to talk about. The game plan is set. Caleb knows exactly what he needs to do to win the game."

But my dad is fixated on Nina. "I— You're saying I'm not relaxed? You're saying I'm stressing out my son? I guess I've stressed him out to the point where he's the number one quarterback in the state as a freshman. How could I possibly do such a thing? How could I possibly behave so terribly?"

"You seem like an amazing dad, Mr. Springer," Nina says. "But you raised your voice, and you slammed the table so hard that I dropped my fork."

My dad blinks a few times. "I do not believe I raised my voice, or that I slammed the table."

"Nina," I say, and she looks at me, and our eyes meet, but I have nothing else to add.

Nina places her napkin on the table. "I'm sorry, I'm being rude. I should go. Caleb, thank you for inviting me. Mr. and Ms. Springer, thank you for having me."

She gets up, and I watch her, and I suddenly panic that she's leaving for good, *forever*, and so before she makes it out of the dining room, I say, "Wait!"

She turns back and waits.

"Why don't you sit back down, hon?" says my mom, but Nina just stands there. Before I can say anything, my dad chimes in.

"It's just as well. You don't need the distraction of a girlfriend right now."

I turn to my dad. "Are you serious? We're freshmen in high school!"

My dad smirks out a laugh. "Listen, Caleb, you're going to break every high school record in this state, and then you're going to win a national championship in college, and then you're going to be a perennial all-pro and win Super Bowls and make a fortune. You're going to have the media breathing down your neck for the rest of your life, watching your every move. You need total focus, and you can't be making any mistakes, especially now, just as it's all beginning."

I see a tear start to fall down Nina's cheek. My dad calling her a "mistake" is what finally gets me to talk.

"I've been thinking, Dad."

"Oh yeah? About what?"

"About football."

My dad harrumphs in triumph. "That's great! It's important to never stop thinking. That's what we're talking about here: game plans, getting every advantage—"

"No, Dad. Not that. Not about the game tomorrow night."

My dad squints for a second, looks at my mom, then back at me. "About what, then?"

"Like, I don't know, the future, in terms of everything you just said about college and the pros and all that stuff." I take a deep breath, hold it in for a few seconds, then let it out slowly. "About whether or not I want to keep playing."

"I don't know what you're—"

I realize there's no turning back now. "I've been thinking about maybe not playing, Dad. Not playing football."

It's so quiet, the only thing you can hear is the grandfather clock in the other room.

"I don't understand, Caleb."

The clock ticks, ticks, ticks.

Nina sits back down and takes my hand under the table. I pause for a second, trying to decide if I should say what I'm about to say.

I decide yes.

"I haven't decided yet, but we all know the truth. It's not safe, Dad. It's not. Look at all the studies. Look at all the ways they keep trying to change the rules."

I glance at my mom, who has tears in her eyes. I turn back to my dad.

"Look at what it's done to you, Dad."

My dad gets up. "Well. Well, well, well. I think we're done here."

My mom stands up, too. "Sammy, honey? I don't want you to overreact. This is just a conversation. We need to be able to be honest with each other, right? We're all dealing with a lot right now, and the game is tomorrow, so let's just—"

"Game?" My dad lets out another joyless laugh. "Game? What game? Your son just announced he's quitting."

"That's not what I said, Dad. Come on."

"I need to go." My dad heads toward the front door.

"Where are you going?" My mom is right behind him. "Sammy, where are you going?"

"I need to take a walk," he says, without looking back.

"We're eating! Please don't walk out now. Honey, please! Let's figure this out."

My dad is calmer now. "I'm sorry, hon. I just—I need to clear my head, think about a few things." He looks back toward me and Nina. "It's all good, Caleb. Seriously. All good. And, Nina, I'm sorry about all this, I truly am. You seem like a nice girl. And a smart girl. Even though you spoke quite rudely to me."

"He doesn't mean that," I whisper to Nina. "It's just the—the—"

"I know, Caleb," Nina says. She's still holding my hand. "I know."

My dad opens the front door. "I won't be long, I promise. Back soon."

But he doesn't come back soon.

He's not back after one hour or two hours or three hours.

He doesn't answer my mom's calls or texts, either.

Nina stays for the first few hours, but then she has to go home. After trying and failing to get some homework done, I plop down on the couch and watch TV. Eventually, my eyes get heavy, but I'm determined to wait up for my dad so I can smooth things over with him before going to bed.

At ten thirty my mom drives to the dealership, but he's not there. At eleven o'clock she calls the police. She tells them that he's missing and that he has dementia. It's the first time I've heard her use that word. She reminds them that they recently found him sleeping at the dealership on top of a car, and then she tells them that my dad has helped raise tens of thousands of dollars for the PAL and the Walthorne Fallen Heroes Fund through his charities and appearances. They tell her that it's too soon to do anything official, but will send out a bulletin and some patrol cars. She gives them a bunch of places my dad likes to go, and they promise they will start looking.

Another hour goes by.

By the time I finally drift off to sleep after midnight, he's still not back.

29

The next morning, I go downstairs and my mom is sitting at the kitchen table, talking to someone on the phone. I can tell by her face that Dad never came home.

She covers the phone to talk to me. "Did you get some sleep?"

"I don't want to go to school," I tell her. "I want to look for Dad."

"You're going to school."

The way she says it makes it clear that she's not in the mood to argue, but I can't help myself. "Why?" I say. "I'm too distracted anyway. And everyone is going to be asking me all about the game and I don't even feel like playing." A decision forms in my head as I'm talking. "If Dad isn't back by game time, I'm definitely not playing."

My mom sighs. "You can't— Let's not worry about the game right now. Your dad will be fine. He's just working some things out. Please go to school, be with your friends, it's where you belong. Dad wouldn't miss this game for the world, you know that."

"Fine."

I was right, of course—at school, all anyone wants to talk about is the game. I see friends in the hall, they tell me to destroy Deaver. My Spanish teacher hands back our quizzes, she tells me I could have done a little better with the verbs, and to beat Deaver. The most popular person in the whole school, a custodian named Frank, sees me in the hall, gives me a high five, and tells me to take it to Deaver.

Meanwhile, Nina is the only one who knows anything about what's going on with my dad. I just don't have the energy to tell anyone else. I don't want to deal with the questions. And I don't have any answers.

At lunch, I'm sitting with Eric and Jamie. Ever since the night at the diner, things haven't been exactly normal between us, even though we're all trying to pretend they have.

"Dude," Eric says to me. "You good?"

"Yeah, why?"

"I don't know, man. You just seem a little . . . off."

"Everything cool?" Jamie adds.

I look at them, my two oldest friends. I want to tell them everything, but I don't know how. So instead, I just say, "You guys . . . listen. I, uh, I know that I haven't been around much this year. I know it's been weird, and hard, and I haven't been all that understanding about it, and that's on me. So yeah, seriously, anyway, I'm real sorry about all that."

"No, no," Eric says. "It's fine. It's all good."

"Totally," Jamie adds.

And then, right on cue, Nina comes over and sits down.

"What's going on?" she asks.

"Caleb was just telling us how sorry he is that he's been a bad friend," Eric says, but he's smiling.

Jamie winks. "We're deciding whether or not to accept his apology."

Nina and the guys laugh, and I try to, too. It's been a lousy day, but seeing the three friends closest to me starting to connect helps me feel a little hopeful.

I decide to text my mom.

anything?

She texts back.

not yet. police are looking.

And just like that, the stress comes flooding back. Without thinking, I slam my phone down. It skids off the table and lands on the floor with a loud clatter.

Eric and Jamie look at me in shock. Kenny, who was just about to join us at the table, bends down to pick up the phone and says, "What the hell?"

We eat quietly for another minute or so, and then the words come tumbling out of my mouth practically without me knowing it. "My dad took off last night. He's missing. We don't know where he is."

My friends stop chewing, stop eating, stop everything.

"Wait, what?" says Eric. "What do you mean, 'missing'?"

"I mean, we got in kind of a fight at dinner last night, and he left, and he hasn't been back since. He's not home, he didn't go to work, no one knows where he is."

Nina leans toward me. "Do these guys know about what's going on with your dad?" she asks, so softly only I can hear it.

I close my eyes for a second and then open them again to see my friends staring at me, waiting. "He's been having some issues lately," I tell them. "Like forgetting stuff, and acting weird. So this is, like, part of that, we think."

I find myself unable to say the word *dementia* out loud.

"Damn, Caleb, I'm so, so sorry," Eric says. "Did you tell Coach? Are people looking for your dad right now?"

I shake my head. "I don't want . . . I mean, uh, no, no one knows. Nina knows because she was at my house last night. I don't want to make a thing out of it. I'm sure he's fine. The police are looking for him. He's fine. I'm just distracted. I don't really feel like playing football right now."

Everyone's eyes go wide.

"We have pregame in two hours," Kenny says.

Pregame is when the team gathers in the locker room and goes over game plans and assignments, before going out onto the field and walking through the first ten plays. Afterward, the coaches give a talk, and we have a buffet meal catered by the booster club. No one eats much. They should really have the buffet after the games, but for some reason they don't.

"When are the buses leaving?" Eric asks.

Kenny and I answer at the same time. "Five thirty."

I don't touch my sandwich, because I'm not hungry. I can feel the whole cafeteria looking at me. Apparently, watching the varsity quarterback eat lunch is the most exciting thing on the planet.

Right now, I would jump off the planet if I could.

“So, you’re gonna play, though, right?” Kenny asks. I see the searching look in his eyes. Almost panic. “You gotta play. Your dad is probably, like, at a bar up in Briscoe right now, getting fired up.” Briscoe is the town where the game is being played. The idea of my dad sitting at a bar up there makes my skin burn.

“I don’t think so,” I say.

“You don’t think what?” Jamie asks. “You don’t think your dad is up there, or you don’t think you’re gonna play?”

“I don’t know! Both!” There’s enough impatience in my voice to make everyone stop talking.

Which is when Nina puts her hand softly on my arm and says, “I think you should play.”

And for the first time all day, I feel something other than confusion and fear.

I feel shock.

“You think what?”

“I think you should play,” she says again. “Your team needs you.”

“Huh? I can’t believe you’re saying this. You, like, hate football! You’ve been—”

"No, she's right," Kenny interrupts. "We need you bad, man."

"Stop, Kenny," I snap, unfairly. "I need to think." I turn back to Nina. "So wait, are you serious?"

She kind of looks like she can't believe what she's saying, but she says it anyway. "You are great at this game, Caleb. I don't know anything about football, and even I can tell. And I know what the game means to you and to your family and to the school and to this whole town. It's one game. You can worry about everything else afterward. And I'll help you figure it out. Your parents will, too. I promise."

"What about my dad—" I start, but Nina shushes me by putting her hand on my cheek.

"I think maybe for the first time ever," she says, "he would agree with me."

And right then I get a text from my mom.

just heard from dad

he's fine and will see us at the game

☺

I feel like a barbell has been lifted off my chest.

I text back:

i love you

Walthorne High vs. Deaver High
State Championship

WWHS
WALTHORNE HIGH SCHOOL RADIO
TRANSCRIPT OF PLAY-BY-PLAY
ALFIE JENKS AND JULIAN HESS

ALFIE: It's a gorgeous night for football! Hi, everyone, I'm Alfie Jenks, coming to you live from Briscoe Stadium, where we're getting set for the high school state championship football game. We've got a great matchup tonight, with the 11–0 Walthorne Wildcats going up against the 10–1 Deaver Warriors. I'm joined as always by my broadcasting partner, Julian Hess, who will highlight some key players for us.

JULIAN: Thanks, broadcasting partner. The Wildcats, of course, are led by their potent attack, with two-time all-state center Ron Johnson in charge of protecting the franchise quarterback Caleb Springer, who led the state in passing yards and touchdowns as a freshman. The Warriors are led by running back Cyrus Washburn and inside linebacker Tim Dockery, both of whom also garnered all-state honors.

ALFIE: Wow, Julian, that was some top-notch broadcasting right there.

JULIAN: Hold up, are you being sarcastic?

ALFIE: Absolutely not.

JULIAN: Sweet! Thanks, Alfie! Let's do this! Yeah, baby, yeah!

ALFIE: Right, uh, let's. The captains meet at midfield for the coin flip . . . Looks like Deaver has won the toss, they will defer, so Walthorne will get the ball first. We'll have a chance right away to see what Caleb Springer and this powerful offense have in store for this huge game . . .

⁜⁜⁜

During the coin toss, I scan the crowd and see Brandon Williams, in a STATE sweatshirt. He nods at me and I nod back. My mom's not here yet. She was at the dealership all day, covering for my dad, and is probably stuck in traffic. I don't see my dad, but that doesn't mean he's not here. Like I said, he likes to hide in the shadows during games.

During kickoff, I try to soak in the atmosphere. *Enjoy this*, I say to myself. *Don't stress. Enjoy it.*

Then the game starts, and it immediately becomes something that's difficult to enjoy. This Deaver team is no joke.

On the very first play we run Popcorn Sizzle Right, which is a play-action pass, slant over the middle. It's the play my dad was warning me about at dinner. I fake the handoff, then flip the ball over the middle to Brett Rose. He hauls in the pass but immediately gets popped by one of their inside linebackers. The ball comes loose, and Deaver recovers.

It only took one play to prove my dad right.

The offense runs to the sideline, where the coaches smack our shoulder pads, trying to pretend they're not furious. They are, of course, but they don't want to scream at us so early in the game, because it would stress us out too much. So they try to be supportive. Brett sits down on the bench by himself. Everyone else is swearing and spitting. We're not used to bad things happening to us on the football field. I know I'm supposed to be upset, but I'm not. I feel okay. Because I see my mom, in the stands, sitting next to Brandon.

She gives me a thumbs-up.

I make a silent promise to my dad, wherever he is.

No more slants.

⁂

ALFIE: What a game this is turning out to be. We're midway through the second quarter, and Deaver is up 14–10. Both teams have been playing good football, and after a costly turnover to start the game, Walthorne has settled down, with quarterback Caleb Springer completing his last seven passes, including a twenty-seven-yard touchdown to senior wideout Brett Rose, who made up for his lost fumble.

JULIAN: But this Deaver team isn't about to roll over and play dead, Alfie—the Walthorne Wildcats are in a dogfight tonight, there's no doubt about it . . .

ALFIE: Can wildcats be in a dogfight?

JULIAN: Hahaha! Alfie made a joke!

ALFIE: Okay then . . .

JULIAN: Good one, Alfie!

ALFIE: Thank you.

JULIAN: Isn't it fun having fun?

ALFIE: It is.

⁘⁘⁘

When I'm in the game, I'm able to concentrate, but every time the defense is on the field, my eyes wander around the stadium.

No sign of my dad.

By the time I hit Brett for a TD, there are six minutes left in the half, and my brain is getting a little twitchy. Deaver has a three and out, which means our offensive is up. I grab Buck, but just as I'm about to run out onto the field, Coach Toffler stops me.

"You good?"

"Yeah, Coach, why?"

"I know about your dad. But he'll be here, Caleb, I'm sure of it. He's so proud of you."

I don't know how he knows, but I don't have time to think about it. "Thank you, Coach."

He looks me in the eye. "I'm going to let you do some play-calling, son. You've earned the right."

"Thank you, Coach."

"Now get out there and make your dad and me both proud."

"Yes, sir, Coach."

I call for an out route, exactly the kind of play my dad was talking about at dinner. He said it would work, and he was right. Ethan Metzger fakes a post pattern, then cuts back outside, I hit him in stride and he takes it all the way down to the Deaver thirty-two yard line. From there, it takes us four plays to score, and we go up 17–14. It's our first lead of the game, and we all breathe a sigh of relief—it seems like we're finally on our way.

"That's what I'm TALKIN' ABOUT!" screams Ron. "They're TOAST! BURNT TOAST!"

Then Deaver runs the kickoff back for a touchdown.

For the first time all season, we're losing at halftime.

⁘⁘⁘

ALFIE: And that's the end of the third quarter, with Deaver holding on to a four-point lead, 35–31. The atmosphere is electric as these two great teams continue to battle. Both offenses have been executing with precision, with Cyrus Washburn accumulating 243 total yards and three touchdowns so far for the Warriors, and Caleb Springer passing for 279 yards and two touchdowns for the Wildcats.

JULIAN: It almost feels like it's going to be one of those games where the last team with the ball wins . . .

⁘⁘⁘

At the beginning of the fourth quarter, I spot Nina. She made it! She's standing to the side of the bleachers, holding her camera. I don't wave to her, but I give a little nod. She nods back and takes my picture.

Normally, seeing her would bring me a feeling of calm, but not tonight. Because I still don't see my dad, and I'm starting to think it's because he's not there. He didn't come after all. I can't believe it. But for some reason, the more shocked I am at the fact that my dad didn't come to the game, the more focused I get on the field.

And it's not just focus. It's anger. It's frustration and confusion and maybe even rage at the fact that I owe everything I am on the football field to my dad, and he's not here to see the most important moment of my football life.

I decide to take it out on the Deaver Warriors.

My passes are sharp. My decision-making is crisp. My legs feel lighter than air as I dance away from the pressure. When I'm in the zone like this, it feels like the game slows down, and I have more time to decide where to go and what to do with the ball. Everyone else feels a step slower as I glide past trouble. It's like a daydream, but with screaming and yelling and stomping and tackling and smashing.

Unfortunately, though, our defense still can't stop their offense. With just over four minutes to go in the game, we're down 45–41, and we have the ball on our own thirty-eight yard line. In the huddle, everyone is jabbering, trying to suggest plays to run, until Ron yells, "SHUT IT! Shut it. The only one who talks is Caleb. He calls the plays! He runs the show." Then he looks at me and nods. "You're the man, Caleb. Lead us down the field so we can whup these guys." Except he doesn't say "guys." He says something much worse.

Ron smacks me on the shoulder pads so hard, it stings. But it's a good sting. After eleven games and most of the twelfth, the captain finally sees me as something more than the golden boy who's easy to make fun of.

He sees me as a leader.

"You got it, Ron," I say. "Flash Whip Forty-Two Bosco." It's a screen pass to Mitch Sellers, our tailback.

We're breaking the huddle when I see a sudden flurry of movement out of the corner of my eye. I turn to see some sort of commotion happening on our sideline—players are scrambling around, the refs are huddling up, coaches are running. All the players on the field are looking, too, and the crowd in the stands rises to their feet. It's that moment that happens sometimes at a game, when a thousand people become one set of eyes, staring at something unusual: two people fighting in the stands or a guy running across the field in his underwear or someone who just had a heart attack.

Except it's none of those things.

It's my dad.

The first thing I notice about my dad is that he's wearing shorts and a T-shirt, even though it's about forty degrees out.

The second thing is how strong and quick he is. People are trying to slow him down, but he's not in the mood to be slowed down.

I look over just as he's sprinting down the sidelines and getting in Coach Toffler's face, screaming at the top of his lungs. "I WANT YOU TO STOP THIS! I WANT YOU TO STOP THIS RIGHT NOW!" Coach is trying to calm my dad as the other assistant coaches clear the players away. I see Brandon Williams and my mom making their way down from the stands, heading straight for my dad, but they're too late. Brandon puts his hand on my dad's shoulder just as a couple of security guys get there, but he ducks out of Brandon's grasp, fakes out the security guys, and starts running out onto the field.

Straight toward our huddle.

The guys see him coming. Ron comes over and stands in front of me, as if to protect me. But my dad runs around him and grabs my arm.

“LET’S GO!” he keeps yelling. “WE’RE LEAVING, CALEB! NOW! LET’S GO!”

I talk softly, trying to keep him calm. “Dad . . . Dad . . . it’s the fourth quarter. I gotta finish this game. C’mon, Dad. This is what we dreamed about, right?”

But there’s no reasoning with him at this point. He shakes his head violently, over and over again, as he rants. “NO! I’VE BEEN THINKING ABOUT IT ALL NIGHT, AND YOU WERE RIGHT! IT’S TOO DANGEROUS! I CAN’T LET YOU PLAY! I CAN’T! LOOK AT ME, CALEB! LOOK AT WHAT HAPPENED TO ME! DO YOU WANT THIS? IS THIS WHAT YOU WANT? IS IT?”

My mom and Brandon are now on the field with us.

“Dinger,” Brandon says, “Dinger, it’s all good. Come on, man. Let the kid finish the game. We got four minutes left. They could win this thing. C’mon, Dinger.”

Brandon gently tries to steer my dad to the sideline, but my dad flicks his hand away and yanks my arm again. “Let’s go, Caleb,” he keeps repeating. “Let’s go.” But his voice has less urgency, less energy. He’s losing steam. I realize that he probably didn’t sleep at all last night.

"Dad, I want to finish the game. The guys are counting on me. Then we can talk about it, I promise. But I need to finish this game."

"You heard him, honey," says my mom. "Caleb's teammates are counting on him. He can't let them down. You never let your teammates down, did you, Sammy?"

"You were the best teammate anyone could ask for, Dinger," adds Brandon. "The best."

"I want to make you proud of me, Dad," I say. "I want to finish this game for my teammates and my school and the whole town and for you."

And then I see it. My dad sags. He sags like teams sag when they know they're done. His shoulders slump and his body softens and the tension in his face melts away, and all that's left is a smaller, sadder man.

He grabs my mom's hand and doesn't let go. Then he turns to me. "Did I ever tell you why they call me Dinger?"

The whole stadium is staring at my dad, waiting to see what he will do next. They can't hear what he's saying, but it seems like they're hanging on every word. Even the referees.

"No, Dad. I mean, I just figured because it rhymes with Springer?"

He points to his head. "It's because of how many times I got dinged."

"Dinged?"

"Knocked in the head, Caleb. Bell rung. Brain-smacked. I got dinged more times than I can count. And every time, some part of me was yelling, 'Enough. Enough.' But another part of me was yelling, 'No. Don't be weak. Your teammates need you. Get back out there.' " He swipes at his eye. "Your teammates will always need you. But the people who love you need you more."

My dad suddenly grabs me and pulls me into him for a hug that nearly knocks the wind out of me. I'm a little bit taller than him, I'm all padded up, but at that moment, folded into his arms, I feel five years old again.

"You go win this game, Caleb, and then we'll talk." He gives me one last squeeze before letting me go and smacking my helmet, very lightly. "Take care of my boy, Buck," he says. "Take care of my boy."

Then he puts his arm around my mom and walks off the field.

WWHS
WALTHORNE HIGH SCHOOL RADIO
TRANSCRIPT OF PLAY-BY-PLAY
ALFIE JENKS AND JULIAN HESS

ALFIE: They couldn't have drawn it up any better, folks. This game has had it all—great offense, some big defensive plays, a few key turnovers, even a bizarre episode when Caleb Springer's famous father disrupted the game for a few minutes, for reasons that we'll have to get to the bottom of later. And now we're all set up for a humdinger of a finish! The Deaver Warriors are clinging to a four-point lead, but Walthorne is sitting with a first and goal at the Deaver eight yard line.

JULIAN: Caleb Springer has been pinpoint perfect on this drive. Especially after the interruption with his dad, he has been playing like a man possessed, completing four passes for forty-three yards and running a quarterback draw that netted sixteen. The only problem is, the clock is showing four seconds left and Walthorne has no time-outs left. There's only time enough for one last play, and they need a touchdown.

ALFIE: The play comes in from the sideline . . . The Wildcats break the huddle, Caleb in the shotgun formation . . . This is for all the marbles, folks . . .

⁂

We're running Freedom Horsepower Right, which basically means I take the shotgun snap, run to the right, and have three options—pass, pitch, or keep. The first option is to hit Amir Watkins, our tight end, who will be cutting across the middle of the end zone. I can also pitch to Mitch Sellers, the tailback, who will be trailing me, or I can run it myself if I see a hole.

Three ways to score, and under a second to decide which one to go for.

I call the signals. "BLUE TWENTY-TWO! BLUE TWENTY-TWO!" I see their inside linebacker sneaking up like he's going to rush, and I holler, "LIGHTNING! LIGHTNING!" which means, *Look out for the blitz!* The fact that the linebacker is blitzing is a good thing, though, because that will open up the middle of the field for Amir, especially if I fake the pitch to Mitch, which might freeze the cornerback.

Like I said, football is complicated.

I yell, “HUT! HUT!” and Ron hikes the ball. I sprint to my right, eyes upfield.

Immediately, I can tell we’re in trouble.

The first thing that goes wrong is that the linebacker who I thought was going to blitz doesn’t blitz. Instead, he drops back into coverage, clogging the middle and blocking the passing lane to Amir.

I silently curse myself for falling into the linebacker’s trap.

The second problem is that behind me, Mitch stumbles as he breaks out of his stance. It’s a fraction of a second, but it’s enough to throw off our timing. Immediately, I lose him as an option.

So, no passing lane, and no pitch option. That leaves the last choice.

I make a run for it.

⁜ ⁜ ⁜

ALFIE: . . . It looks like Springer is going to keep the ball . . . The clock is winding down to zero . . . He makes the first guy miss . . . Ron Johnson makes a crushing block . . . Springer breaks a tackle at the five . . . heading toward the corner flag . . . Oh, the safety comes flying in and makes a tremendous hit! Springer is staggered as he pushes forward . . . He takes another hit and his head hits the turf hard as tacklers pile on . . . Hard to say from this angle whether the ball crossed the goal line . . . We're waiting for the official signal from the referee . . .

⁘⁘⁘

After I break a couple of tackles right at the line of scrimmage to gain the first few yards, Ron lays the massive hit on one of the safeties, and I think I'm home free. But the other safety comes out of nowhere and drives right into my gut.

That's when I become what football players call a "wounded buffalo." Someone who is staggered, slowed down, easy prey for all the other hunters smelling blood and looking for fresh meat.

At about the three yard line, I become fresh meat.

The other defenders swarm me, hit me high and low, trying to punch the ball out and cause a fumble, sticking their fingers through my face mask to gouge my eyes, piling on, three, four, five guys. On the other side, Ron, Kenny, and the other linemen are fighting them off, trying to help push me into the end zone. Eventually, I'm buried by people on both teams, probably about 1,500 pounds of human flesh on top of me, pushing, pulling as I drive my legs forward, forward, into the end zone, into a state championship, into the record books, into the end of this season that has been amazing and awesome and terrifying and exhausting.

And then the weight becomes too much and my legs collapse, and I fall, and the bodies fall on top of me, and I brace for impact against the turf, the hard turf, the turf that can feel like concrete sometimes.

And Buck tries to do his job, tries to protect me, but the first thing that hits the turf is my head, which slams down hard.

HARD.

And there it is again—the same feeling I got when I took that first massive hit of the season, way back in the opening game. I recognize it all: the bright lights through closed eyes, the colors shooting around my head, the buzzing, the loud breathing that seems like it's coming from far away until I realize it's me.

I feel it all.

And then the world slowly comes back into focus, the noise, and someone is helping me up, and someone is lifting me up, onto their shoulders, and people are screaming, and it takes me a few seconds to realize it's happy screaming, and I begin to figure out what happened, and it seems like I'm the last to know.

I scored.

We won.

It's over.

◂30

I don't know if the ringing in my ears is from the hit or the noise.

Or both.

The ringing is there as people from the stands rush onto the field, swarming me, smacking me on the back, the shoulders, the arms, grabbing me, trying to high-five me

The ringing is there as Eric and Jamie reach me, and they jump on me, yelling "Bro, you are the MAN!" over and over again, no jealousy, no resentment, just pure excitement and joy, and I'm so grateful that they're my best friends

The ringing is there as Ron gives me a bear hug that squeezes what little air is left in my lungs as he yells, "Dude, you are a SUPERSTAR"

The ringing is there as I spot Nina, and try to run toward her even though my legs aren't really working, and she jumps into my arms so hard I almost fall, and I say, "You made it," and she says, "You did it you did it you did it," over and over, and I say, "My head hurts," and she says, "It's okay, I know, it's okay," and I whisper to her, "*It's not about me, It's not about you,*

It's about us," and she starts crying and says, "That's my song, you're singing my song," and I start crying, too, and say, "Well, I wouldn't say singing, exactly," and we both laugh through our tears

It's there as Brandon Williams shakes my hand, his grip strong, my grip not, but he doesn't care, he's talking about me coming back up to State to see the conference playoff, they're hoping for a bowl bid, I hear some of the words but not all of the words, but I nod, "Yeah, yeah, I can't wait"

It's there as my mom reaches me and immediately tries to shield me from the mob, like a lion protecting her cub, and I say, "I hit my head, Ma," and she wants to get me out of there, she can tell I'm a little wobbly, but it's kind of a madhouse, so she does the best she can

The ringing is there as I look and look and look and then see him, my dad, alone, and I think he's waiting for me to come to him, like everyone always does, including me, but this time it's different, this time it's the reverse, this time he's moving toward me, he's coming to me, and his face is a jumble, I see pride, I see pain, I see confusion, I see worry, I see joy, I see guilt, or maybe I don't really see any of those things, maybe those are the feelings inside me, but either way, I see my dad, and I see myself in my dad

And he pulls me into him and says, "I'm so proud of you, Caleb"

And I bury my head in his shoulder and say, "I'm so proud of you, too, Dad"

The ringing is there as we stop hugging and he pulls back and looks at me, he knows I got hit, and he says, "That kid really popped you there. You okay?"

And that's when I realize I still have my helmet on, I had it on this whole time, and I pull it off and say, "Yeah, Dad, I mean, I think so, I hope so"

But of course I have no idea

No one has any idea, really

And that's when I have a different idea

And I say to my dad, "I'll be right back"

He says, "Okay, son, I love you"

I say, "I love you, too, Dad"

And while the joy and the celebration and the chaos is still all around me, surrounding me, I walk back onto the field, past the high-fivers and the news cameras and the coaches drenched in Gatorade and the students who have their shirts off even though it's freezing out, and I head toward the fifty yard line, and it's almost like a miracle but no one follows me, so finally, I'm alone, and the noise fades into the background, and I take a knee, and I place my helmet down on the field, right on the fifty

And I lean down and whisper, "See you around, Buck"

And I stand up, and I look over at the celebrating crowd, and I think about the sport that has been at the center of my life ever since I can remember

And I start to walk back to everyone I love, and they see me coming, everyone smiling and together and ready to take on whatever comes

And that's when the ringing stops.

AUTHOR'S NOTE

When I started working on *Game Changer* (my previous Walthorne football novel) some five years ago, I wanted to write a book that people assumed was about concussions, brain injuries, and the dangers of playing football. Only after finishing the story would readers discover it was really about the culture of the game, off the field as much as on. But with *Dinged*, I felt it was time to directly approach the helmeted elephant in the room: the fact that so many Americans (including myself) continue to enjoy and support a popular form of American entertainment—in fact, perhaps *the* most popular form of American entertainment—that so obviously has very real and sometimes life-threatening risks for its participants of all ages.

Readers may know that my youngest son, Jack, played football through high school. With him, I knew the danger that existed, but my wife and I did some parental calculations and decided that his love of the game (and my love of watching him) outweighed the risk of him suffering serious injury. And luckily, we were right. Then for a minute there, it looked like Jack might continue to play in college, which would have meant a whole new set of calculations, with perhaps a different outcome. It turned out that we did not have to make that decision, but it got me thinking: How do parents and families deal with such a dilemma? Especially if the child does not just love the game, but has a rare talent for it? That seemed like conflict enough—then add in a father, himself a former star player who is now suffering terrible health issues as a result of playing, and you have a recipe for some absorbing, thought-provoking drama.

A lot of people have written to me over the last few years asking why there wasn't a sequel to *Game Changer*. My answer was always the same—it seemed like that particular story was complete, even if Teddy Youngblood's own journey was just beginning. But *Dinged* could certainly be considered a continuation of sorts. It, too, addresses questions that I, frankly, have no answers for: Why do we still love football? Why do *I* still love football? What can we do to make sure that those who play the game are as safe as possible? And knowing that it's *not* possible to make every player safe all the time, is it acceptable to continue to go to the high school stadium on Friday night, or turn on the TV every Saturday or Sunday or Monday night and watch and cheer and enjoy?

The last thing I want to do with this book is tell readers what to think. I only want to *encourage* them to think. That's the gift of complicated subjects and compelling storytelling.

Hopefully, I've done my part with the storytelling.

The rest is up to you!

RESOURCES

Here are some interesting articles that touch upon the themes and subjects in this book:

cdc.gov/traumaticbraininjury/pubs/youth_football_head_impacts.html
beingpatient.com/concussions-youth-football
nytimes.com/2021/10/14/sports/catholic-church-football-concussions.html
parents.com/kids/safety/sports/should-you-let-your-kid-play-football-experts-weigh-in

You'll notice that the book is dedicated to the memory of Mike Webster. Here's a little more about Mike, who was the first athlete (posthumously) diagnosed with brain trauma directly attributed to playing in the NFL:

wikipedia.org/wiki/Mike_Webster
theatlantic.com/health/archive/2015/12/the-nfl-players-brain-that-changed-the-history-of-the-concussion/417597
sportshistorynetwork.com/football/nfl/mike-webster

ACKNOWLEDGMENTS

Thank you to Erica Finkel for invaluable guidance, as always.

Thank you to Emily, Jenny, Brooke, Kathy, Megan, Chelsea, Deena, Maggie, Andrew, Kim, Hallie, Trish, Jody, Elisa, and everyone at Abrams for being such great teammates on these books.

Thank you to Amy Thrall Flynn and Rubin Pfeffer for stepping in and stepping up.

And thank you to all the athletes, medical professionals, coaches, and parents for continuing the work. It's not easy navigating the balance between the pleasures and the perils of one of the world's greatest sports, while trying to make things better—but one thing I know for sure is that at long last, everyone is trying.